Ellie, ENGINEER

In the Spotlight

Also by Jackson Pearce

The Doublecross

The Inside Job

Ellie, Engineer

Ellie, Engineer: The Next Level

Ellie, ENGINEER In the Spotlight

JACKSON PEARCE

ILLUSTRATED BY
TUESDAY MOURNING

BLOOMSBURY
CHILDREN'S BOOKS
NEW YORK   LONDON   OXFORD   NEW DELHI   SYDNEY

BLOOMSBURY CHILDREN'S BOOKS
Bloomsbury Publishing Inc., part of Bloomsbury Publishing Plc
1385 Broadway, New York, NY 10018

BLOOMSBURY, BLOOMSBURY CHILDREN'S BOOKS, and the Diana logo
are trademarks of Bloomsbury Publishing Plc

First published in the United States of America in November 2019
by Bloomsbury Children's Books

Bloomsbury books may be purchased for business or promotional use. For information on
bulk purchases please contact Macmillan Corporate and Premium Sales Department at
specialmarkets@macmillan.com

Library of Congress Cataloging-in-Publication Data
Names: Pearce, Jackson, author.
Title: Ellie, engineer : in the spotlight / by Jackson Pearce.
Other titles: In the spotlight
Description: New York : Bloomsbury, 2019.
Summary: When Kit's pageant rival Melody loses her rabbit, Ellie believes she can
build a contraption to catch him, but she begins to doubt herself when Melody
insists that a pageant is no place for messy engineering experiments.
Identifiers: LCCN 2019022391 (print) | LCCN 2019019802 (e-book)
ISBN 978-1-5476-0185-1 (hardcover) • ISBN 978-1-5476-0186-8 (e-book)
Subjects: | CYAC: Engineering—Fiction. | Building—Fiction. | Pageants—Fiction. |
Sex role—Fiction. | Self-perception—Fiction.
Classification: LCC PZ7.P31482 Elp 2019 (e-book) | LCC PZ7.P31482 (print) | DDC [Fic]—dc23
LC record available at https://lccn.loc.gov/2019022391

Book design by Jeanette Levy
Typeset by Westchester Publishing Services
Printed and bound in the U.S.A. by Berryville Graphics Inc., Berryville, Virginia
2 4 6 8 10 9 7 5 3 1

All papers used by Bloomsbury Publishing Plc are natural, recyclable
products made from wood grown in well-managed forests. The manufacturing processes
conform to the environmental regulations of the country of origin.

To find out more about our authors and books visit www.bloomsbury.com
and sign up for our newsletters.

For Blueberry,
who is destined to have
a great many
engineering skills

Ellie, ENGINEER

In the Spotlight

Chapter One

Ellie Bell was standing at the very, very edge, looking over.

It wasn't a terribly high edge, but it was *not* something she wanted to fall off. It was definitely not something she wanted to *skateboard* off, even though she'd designed and built it for exactly that purpose—Project 71: Fold-up! Light-up! Skateboard Ramp!

(She put lots of exclamation points in this project title, since she felt like it was extra exciting.)

Ellie wasn't the skateboarder, though—Kit was. And Kit looked *very* ready to skateboard right off the edge, down the ramp, then up the other side.

"Here goes!" Kit said excitedly, rapping on her bright-pink helmet to make sure it was in place. Kit's skateboard was pink, too, except for the purple otters she'd drawn on the underside, and so were her kneepads and wrist guards. Kit liked pink basically as much as Ellie liked purple, which was a *lot*. Ellie held a rectangle-shaped battery in one hand and the end of the wire of string lights in the other. The lights went all around the edges of the ramp and down the middle. It was the first time she'd ever built something with lights on it before! Ellie wrapped the end of the wire around the little circle on the end of the battery, and the lights instantly lit up.

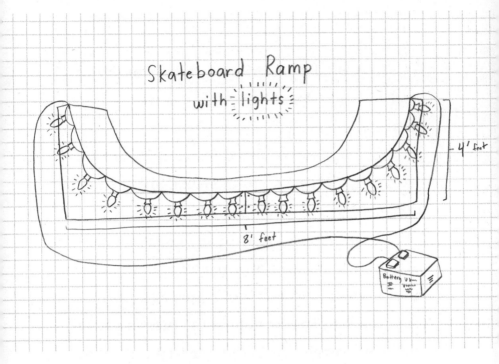

Skateboard Ramp
with lights

4' feet

8' feet

Battery ∨box

"If you fall, I know how to stabilize your leg until the ambulance arrives!" their friend Toby called from the far side of the driveway, looking very serious. Toby knew how to do all sorts of stuff like this, though sometimes it was more helpful than other times. He went on. "At least, I do if I can find a stick. Maybe you should wait to go until I can find a good stick?"

"I think I'll just risk it, but thanks!" Kit called back. And then with a clatter and a *whoosh*, she pushed off the edge!

Kit flew forward, down the ramp, knees bent and skirt fluffing up in the wind. She reached the bottom of the ramp and then started back up the other side, toward the opposite edge. Ellie threw her hands in the air and whooped as Kit and her skateboard launched right into the sky. Kit grabbed hold of the edge and held it for a moment, then she released it seconds before the skateboard hit the ground again with her feet planted right in the middle. Kit skated back down the far side of the ramp, back toward the middle, up, and—

"*Oof!*" Kit said as she pitched forward.

Ellie yelped.

Toby shouted, "I'll find a stick!"

But Kit knew how to fall off a skateboard—she'd done it plenty of times, after all, since that was how learning to skateboard worked. Kit tucked her arms in and rolled. In a split second, she was on her feet without a single scratch. The skateboard whizzed back and forth as it slowed down, then it finally stopped right in the middle of the ramp.

"Are you okay?" Ellie said, running up to Kit, even though she could already tell Kit was just fine.

"Yep!" Kit said cheerfully. "I think my wheels got caught on the lights," she added, then guided Ellie over to a spot near the top of the ramp. Her board had indeed gotten hung up on the string of lights and snapped it into two pieces. "Oh no! I broke them!" Kit realized, putting a hand to her mouth.

"It's all right," Ellie said. "You just broke the road."

"That doesn't sound all right," Kit answered, shaking her head.

"It is! See, look," Ellie said, and pointed at the place where the string of lights was snapped. "To make the lights turn on, the electricity has to go in a circle—that's why it's called an electrical *circuit*. *Circ*le, *circ*uit, get it? Anyway—you just smashed up part of the road, like the Godzilla monster did in that movie we weren't supposed to watch. All we have to do is fix the break in the road, and then the electricity can go round and round in the circuit again."

Kit didn't seem convinced.

"Watch," Ellie said, and took the broken ends of the string lights. She carefully twisted the bits of broken wire back together and *ta-da*, the lights blinked back on.

Before

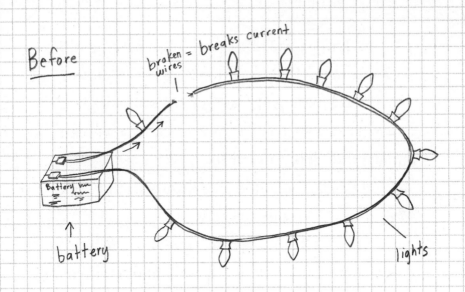

broken = breaks current
broken wires

battery

lights

After

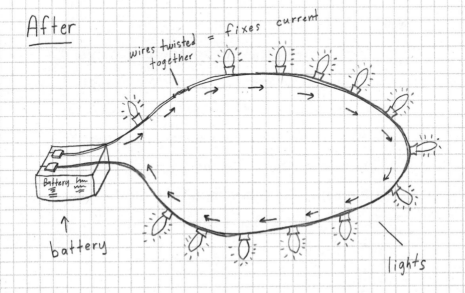

wires twisted together = fixes current

battery

lights

"I have a stick!" Toby said, panting up beside them. He was clutching a stick that was three times as long as Kit's leg and still had a pine cone attached. "It's long, but we can maybe cut it to fit your leg."

"I don't think I'll need it after all, but thank you, Toby," Kit said politely.

"Oh. Well, maybe we should keep it by the ramp, just in case," Toby said, trying not to look *too* disappointed that Kit's leg didn't need stabilizing. Toby really liked putting his research to good use. "Anyway, what happened? The lights broke?"

"Kit's wheels caught the wire and snapped it, so the circuit broke. It's fixed now, though—I think the light string was just too loose, so it got all snarled easily—we ought to tighten the string up so there isn't any extra," Ellie said. "And maybe the lights should go on the sides instead of the top? But . . . hmm . . . that'll make it harder to fold up . . ."

Kit frowned. "If it doesn't fold up, it won't fit in my mom's car."

"Maybe I could put wheels on it, and we could *attach* it to your mom's car, and then we can *tow* it to the Miss Junior Peachy Clean Pageant!" Ellie said, eyes going big like capital "O's." It wouldn't be *that* hard to find wheels, would it? As long as Kit's mom drove very slowly—

"I thought it was the Miss Junior Pecan *Queen* Pageant," Toby said, interrupting her thinking.

"It's the Miss Peachy *Keen* Pageant," Kit corrected them both. "And that's a really good idea, Ellie, but I don't think my mom will let us attach anything to her car again. She made a rule about it, remember?"

"Oh. Right," Ellie said, frowning. Kit's mom made a lot of rules—there were the regular rules that most adults had, like the "inside voices" rule and the "no muddy shoes on the couch" rule, but then she also had a lot of rules that were made mostly for when Ellie was around, like the "butter is for bread not robot parts" rule and the "no jumping off anything higher than three feet no matter what sort of parachute / bungee cord / rope you have attached" rule. She'd made the "leave my car out of it" rule after Ellie and Kit had used her car to launch a kite into the air. Ellie thought it was pretty unfair, since the car had worked as a *great* kite launcher; it just turned out to not be such a great kite *flyer* when she drove under a stoplight, and the kite got caught and then fell onto the windshield, and Kit's mom thought it was a parrot attacking the car, and—

Well. It really wasn't all *that* bad in the end, but Kit's mom seemed to think it was.

"All right, let's think," Ellie said. "If we could put the lights on *after* we get to the pageant, that might work. But then they still have to get folded up to go to the stage, right? I wish they'd just let us put the lights together *on* the stage. That'd be best."

"Ooh, and if they *did* let you do that, that could be your talent, Ellie!" Toby said helpfully.

Ellie shook her head. "I just don't think that would be a good pageant talent."

Kit had begged Ellie to enter the Miss Peachy Keen pageant with her, and because Kit almost always did things that Ellie wanted, Ellie had agreed. Even better, Toby was going to come along with them, too. He wasn't going to be in the pageant, but his mom thought a weekend at a pretty hotel with Kit's and Ellie's moms would be fun.

The only catch was that this would be the very first time Ellie was *ever* going to be in a pageant, and she was pretty nervous. Fluffing her hair big and wearing lipstick didn't worry her—she liked lipstick, after all, and the way it left kissy marks when you kissed your arm or your electric drill or the wall—but the talent part had her feeling squiggly. Ellie knew what her best talent was—it was engineering!— but after doing a little research, Ellie had decided that engineering wasn't a good pageant talent. As best as Ellie could tell, pageant talents were supposed to be flashy and fancy and loud—like singing or dancing or, in Kit's case, skateboarding.

"Or maybe I can teach you to stabilize bones! If Kit breaks her leg, your talent will be *really* impressive," Toby said.

"I don't want to count on breaking my leg, though, Ellie, if you don't mind," Kit said.

"I don't think I have permission to break mine," Toby said with a shrug.

"It's okay. I'm just going to do my ballet routine," Ellie said. "But maybe you can teach me how to stabilize bones, Toby, just in case. You're right—that would be a really impressive talent."

"Yes!" Toby said, cheering.

"But before we start fixing bones—maybe I can try the ramp again? It'll get dark soon," Kit said. "I want it to be perfect for the pageant!"

Ellie gave her a thumbs-up. "Don't worry at all, Kit—the pageant people aren't going to know what hit them!"

Chapter Two

"Look at what I added!" Ellie's mom said that night, holding up a dress that was very purple and very fluffy. It took Ellie a minute to figure out what her mom was talking about, but then she saw it—a new ruffly bit right by the bottom of the skirt.

"That looks great!" Ellie said. Ellie's mom knew how to sew but didn't really know how to *stop* sewing. Last week, she announced that she'd "officially finished" Ellie's dress, but every night since then she'd been adding ruffles and straps and skirts and beads and sequins. Ellie didn't mind, though, since she liked all those things and hardly ever got to wear them all at once.

"You know what, though? Now this area looks sparse. Doesn't it look sparse?" Ellie's mom asked, waving her hand around the middle of the skirt.

"Very sparse," Ellie agreed. Her mom grinned, then grabbed some giant sequins off a nearby Styrofoam plate. Ellie took the plate, emptied the rest of the sequins off onto the bed, then grabbed for another Styrofoam plate—it was already empty. Ellie didn't know what had originally been on it, but based on how many ruffles were on the pageant dress, she guessed ribbons.

Ellie put one plate facedown on the floor, then used a scrap of fabric to rub the top of it. Then she put the second plate up against it—

The second plate swooshed away! Ellie grinned, then did it again. Each time, the second plate swooshed off, like it couldn't stand to be so close to the plate on the ground.

"Look!" Ellie called to her mom. "I have magic powers!"

"Magic powers?" Ellie's mom said without turning around. "What sort of powers?"

"I can make these plates angry with each other, see?" Ellie said. Her mom turned to look just as one plate swooshed away. Ellie grinned. "It's not really magic. It's just the static electricity."

"Rats. I was hoping for magical pizza-conjuring powers. Or at least cold soda-conjuring powers," Ellie's mom said, pretending to be disappointed.

"It's static because it stays still—the electricity stays right here between the plates," Ellie said. "It's different from the electricity

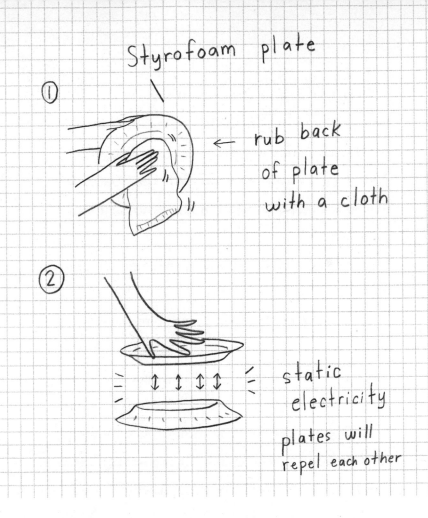

Styrofoam plate

①

← rub back
of plate
with a cloth

②

static
electricity

plates will
repel each other

that goes through wires, like the ones for the
lights on Kit's skateboard ramp, because that's
electric *current*. It moves through the wires.
Kinda like a river has a current, you know?"

"Or like how a can of soda could *currently* be on its way to me," Ellie's mom said.

"It's the same as when you rub a balloon on your head," Ellie went on. "All the electricity just sits in one place and makes your hair stand up all crazy."

"You know what would be *crazy* good? A can of soda," Ellie's mom said.

Ellie blinked. "Would you like me to get you a can of soda?" she asked.

"How did you know?" Ellie's mom said happily. "Yes, please."

Ellie went downstairs and got her mom the soda. When she returned, all the sequins that had been on the bed (and the Styrofoam plate before that) were now on her pageant dress. That one area definitely didn't look sparse now.

"Perfect!" Ellie's mom said, and opened the soda before giving Ellie a sip. "Hey, maybe you could tell people about static electricity for your talent! That is, if you still aren't sure about doing your ballet routine from the spring recital?"

Ellie sighed and flopped onto the bed, sending bits of thread and sequins into the air and back down, like glitter rain. "I *like* my ballet routine; I just know it isn't my best talent. Engineering is!"

Ellie's mom frowned. "Well, that's true—you are very good at engineering. But you are a very good ballet dancer, too! Do you know many of the other contestants' talents? Maybe looking at those will give us some new ideas."

Ellie knew only that lots of contestants sang and danced, so she and her mom looked at the Miss Peachy Keen Pageant website and found the page where all the contestants were listed. There were twenty-five girls entered in the category that Ellie and Kit were in—Miss Junior Peachy Keen—and each had a few pictures and some things about them written on the page. Lots of the girls—like Kit—had very fancy pictures of them wearing real lipstick and dangly earrings. Ellie's entry didn't have much written about her, but she liked her picture—it was right after she'd lost a tooth, and it made her smile look funny *strange* and maybe a little funny *ha-ha*.

"Let's see—singing, singing, singing," Ellie's mom said, reading up on each contestant. "Ooh, this girl juggles! That's a fun talent."

"Ooh, I bet I could build a machine to toss her those clubs, so she doesn't have to have someone else do it!" Ellie said, pointing to someone she guessed was the girl's mother—who was mid-club toss—in the photo.

"That would be a very nice thing to offer, but perhaps there's not enough time for *this* pageant," Ellie's mom said. "This girl plays the violin, and oh—this girl plays the flute *while* she dances!"

"Whoa!" Ellie said. "That's such a good talent!" She grabbed one of her pigtails and pulled it. How was she supposed to go on after jugglers and singers and Kit's skateboarding and flute playing while dancing? She had to come up with something amazing!

"This girl does a magic act," Ellie's mom said, scrolling along.

"Hey, I know who that is!" Ellie answered, pouncing toward the computer screen. "That's Melody Harris!"

"Does she go to your school?" Ellie's mom asked, tilting her head at the girl's picture. Melody Harris had dark-brown hair and big eyes. She was wearing a sparkly necklace and sparkly earrings and a sparkly bracelet, which you could see because she had her chin propped up on her hand for her picture. She was even wearing nail polish, and Ellie would have bet her favorite hammer it wasn't the peel-off kind.

Ellie shook her head. "Nope. I don't really *know* her—I just know her name. She and Kit are always in pageants together."

"Oh, that's nice!"

Ellie kept shaking her head. "Nope again. Melody and Kit don't get along because Melody doesn't like it when Kit wins."

"What about when Melody wins?"

"Melody probably really likes that."

"I meant what does *Kit* think when Melody wins, Ellie?" her mom asked pointedly.

Ellie shrugged. "I don't think losing the pageant bothers Kit as much as people not getting along does." Kit hated fights and arguing and people being left out, even if they weren't *actually* being left out but were just trying to sneak up on a lizard, and Kit accidentally scared it away by shouting, "Hello! I'm Kit! What's your name?" (This happened to a new boy at school. He forgave Kit, but it took a little while, since it'd been an especially big lizard.)

"Well, Melody's magic act does look very impressive. I can see why she wins a lot of pageants," Ellie's mom said, looking back at the screen. There was a picture of Melody Harris in a shiny magician's tuxedo with a red bow tie. She had a top hat in one hand, and popping out of it was a real live rabbit with white fur.

Ellie thought hard. "Maybe for my talent, I can build a rabbit tunnel, except one that's like an ant farm. You know, where you can see in one side? And then the audience can watch the rabbit crawl through the tunnel!"

"That sounds *very* cool, but it doesn't sound like Melody would let you borrow her rabbit. Besides, you only have two and a half minutes for your talent," Ellie's mom reminded her in a gentle voice. "And you know what takes *exactly* two and a half minutes? Your ballet routine," Ellie's mom said with a grin, then turned back to her sewing machine.

Chapter Three

"I *love* pageants!" Toby said. Or at least, that's what Ellie guessed he said—his mouth was full of chocolate candy.

"Me too!" Ellie answered. Or at least, that's what she tried to say—her mouth was also full of chocolate candy.

"Be careful—the judges are already watching! They're *always* watching," Kit told them both. Her mouth was not full of candy; she ate the M&M's in her palm one at a time, looking very pretty as she did so. Kit was always better at these types of things than Ellie.

Ellie swallowed her candy and tried to stand up a little straighter; Kit gave her a thumbs-up. They were at the hotel, and at the Miss Peachy Keen Pageant check-in desk, there was an enormous table *covered* in candy. It was arranged in pretty rows of dishes that sat on top of mint-green cardboard heart cutouts, and almost all the candy was peach or white or mint green. Even the M&M's were those colors, even though they still all just tasted like regular chocolate.

Ellie's and Kit's moms were signing lots of forms and shuffling lots of papers around, while Toby's mom got the key cards to their hotel rooms from the front desk. They hurried to put Kit's skateboarding ramp in a big ballroom just next to the one the pageant itself would be held in, then rushed up to their hotel rooms to put on swimsuits. This hotel was not only home to the Miss Peachy Keen Pageant; it was also home to a *very* cool swimming pool with a giant dragon statue that had three different diving boards in it—one from the foot, one from its back, and then one super high one on the dragon's tongue. That was the *best* one, since in the pictures of the hotel, it looked like the dragon was reverse-eating people as they jumped off it.

"I *seriously* love pageants!" Toby whooped as soon as they stepped into the pool area. It was just the right amount of hot outside—the amount that made you want to get in the pool but not so hot that it made you want to stay inside all day. Toby led the charge up to the dragon's tongue diving board. There was a big, winding staircase that swirled up, up, up to the dragon's head, and there was a little line of people taking their turns being reverse-eaten as they jumped into the water below.

"Oh," Toby said when he got to the top. There was a lifeguard by the entrance of the diving board. She had a very nice face and a big ponytail, and she smiled at Toby.

"Ready?" the lifeguard asked.

"Oh," Toby said again, but didn't move.

Ellie frowned and stepped a bit closer to Toby. She suddenly understood why he wasn't moving. The dragon's head was *much* higher than it looked from the ground. Ellie didn't know if Toby was afraid of heights, but she knew that she *wasn't*, and even her stomach felt kind of floppy.

"What's wrong?" Kit whispered from behind Ellie—she couldn't see over the edge just yet.

"Nothing!" Ellie said quickly, but she made eyes at Kit that said, *Something.* Kit made eyes back that said, *Oh, okay,* and then nodded. They were good at eye talking—most best friends were.

"What's taking so long?" a stranger asked—it was a boy behind Kit. Before Ellie could answer, *another* kid came up behind that boy. The line was starting to get backed up.

"We're doing an experiment!" Ellie said quickly. "It's important."

"We are?" Toby asked without looking back at Ellie.

"Yep. So I was doing some research—" Ellie turned back to look at the new kids in the line, thinking fast. "I'm an engineer, see. Anyway, I was doing some research on how to make the biggest splash in the water."

"Easy—cannonball. Can I go if he won't?" one of the girls in line asked impatiently.

"Don't be rude; she's explaining something," Kit said in a very grown-up voice, and the girl went quiet.

"The splash comes from how you *kapow* the water out of its place when you hit it. It's called *displacement*."

"I know about displacement!" Toby said suddenly, looking over his shoulder. Ellie grinned at him—he looked a little less scared and a little more curious, just like Ellie had hoped.

"Then you know that the biggest splash comes from displacing the most water. But how do you do it? You can cannonball, but do you go in butt first? Or back first? Or head first?"

"Maybe it all depends on the size of your butt," the lifeguard said thoughtfully. All the kids looked at her, and she shrugged. "I'm just saying."

"Right, well, I think we should work together to figure out how to make the biggest splash. I'm going to jump and hit butt first, then start swimming up as fast as I can. Kit, you hit butt first, but then wait until you go deeper to break the cannonball shape and start swimming."

"I'll go back first!" the girl who had been in a rush before said.

butt first

traditional dive

back first

knees first

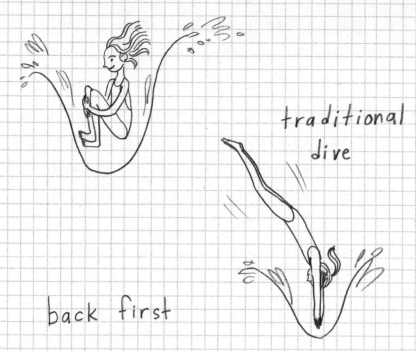

"I can do a flip before I hit the water, prob- ably! And if not, it'll be head first! Again!" the boy in line said eagerly. Everyone looked excited, and Ellie really wished she could swim with her tool belt on—or at least, that she'd brought her notepad to the pool. This *was* good research, even if it was mostly just to make Toby feel better.

"What should I do?" Toby asked. He still looked a little scared, but now he also looked *excited*. Toby really liked engineering, now that Ellie had taught him so much about it.

"You're the *control* this time," Ellie said. "That means you just jump however you want, and we'll compare that splash to the other splashes. You can't go wrong!"

"Oh, good!" Toby said. He turned back around and stared down the end of the drag- on's tongue. It was still really high, but now, it wasn't about being reverse-eaten by a dragon.

It was about *research*. Toby took a deep breath, ran forward, and flung himself off the board. Ellie and Kit rushed to the edge; the lifeguard poked her head between them to watch him fall.

It was just about the furthest thing from a cannonball possible. His arms were out, his legs were kicking, and he was yelling, "Ooooaaaaaaooooohhhh!" like he was sort of Tarzan but also sort of a ghost. He splashed into the water, and a moment later, he came back to the surface.

"Did you see it? Do you know how big the splash was?" he shouted up at Ellie as he doggie-paddled over to the ladder.

"Yes! Got it! I'm going to call it a two!" Ellie said, then turned to Kit with a frown. "Though really, we should probably measure the height of the splash *and* the width, don't you think? I only looked at the width that time—he splashed all the way to those first lines on the bottom of the pool. Hmm—" Ellie was still hmm-ing as she walked to the end of the board and jumped off, pulling her knees up to her chest and cannon-balling into the pool. The water was cold and ran into her ears, and when she huffed back up to the top, she whooped as loud as she could.

"That was great! You almost splashed me!" Toby said from the side of the pool. "Kit, you go!" he shouted, and Kit nodded, then cannon-balled into the water with a splash that Ellie gave a six on her splash scale. Then the back-first girl did a five, and the boy (who tried to flip but *did* end up splashing headfirst) did a four.

"This is great!" Ellie said. "Okay, let's all go again and try a new way. And we probably need to find some more people, too!"

"I'll go find people with different-size butts!" Toby shouted helpfully.

The girl jumped up and down and clapped her hands. "I'll help! My mom's butt is—"

"*Excuse me,*" a voice said. It wasn't the sort of "excuse me" you say when you're squeezing past someone in the grocery store or when you need help at the counter of the gas station but you're too small for the clerk to see you. It was the sort of "excuse me" that was an *order* not a question.

Ellie turned around, wet hair flipping across her eyes like a clump of seaweed. She shook it off and then looked up to see a very, very tall and very, very serious-looking lady with her arms folded across her chest. She had dark-brown hair and big eyes and looked *just* like a grown-up version of the little girl who was standing beside her—a little girl who Ellie recognized from pictures.

It was Melody Harris, the girl with the magic-act talent. The girl who was Kit's biggest rival. And right now, a girl who did *not* look happy.

Chapter Four

"Hello, Melody! How are you today?" Kit said brightly.

"I am *wet*," Melody said stiffly. "*Someone* decided to have a splash contest *at the pool*."

Ellie wondered where else people were supposed to have splash contests but didn't say anything.

"I hope all the splashing is quite finished,"

the woman—Melody's mother, Ellie was sure—said. "We are trying to *relax*."

"I want to make sure I'm fully refreshed for tomorrow," Melody added tartly. "And besides, who knows *what's* in that pool water. It's terrible for your hair."

Toby piped up. "I know what's in the pool water! It's chlorine! It kills all the germs in the pool. It's important, since some people pee in the pool."

"Oh, that's true," Ellie said, nodding.

Melody looked horrified, then turned to Kit. "Katherine, *who* are these people?"

Kit smiled, even though she didn't really like it when people called her "Katherine" instead of just "Kit." "These are my friends! This is Ellie Bell, and this is Toby Michaels."

Ellie added, "I'm going to be in the Miss Peachy Keen Pageant with you!"

"I've told you about her before, Melody. Ellie is my friend the engineer!" Kit added.

"Oh," Melody said, her eyebrows lifting like Kit had said a bad word. "An *engineer*? So you drive a train?"

"That's a different sort of engineer," Ellie said. "I build things."

"Oh," Melody said again, crinkling her nose.

"We were just doing an experiment to find out what kind of cannonball makes the best splash," Toby jumped in. "Do you want to help?"

"Absolutely not," Melody said, and straightened the straps on her bright-purple swimsuit. It wasn't even the tiniest bit wet—Ellie wondered if it had ever even been in the water. "Engineering looks messy. And if you're quite finished, we'd like to go back to relaxing instead of being *splashed*."

"I understand," Kit said politely. "We'll try to keep from splashing you, Melody. Good luck tomorrow."

"*Thank you*," Melody said, and then she and her mom spun around in unison. They walked back to two pool chairs, lowered their sunglasses, and lay down. It all looked like a super-boring way to spend an afternoon at a pool, especially when you could be reverse-eaten by a dragon. In fact, it all seemed pretty silly to Ellie. A pool was for swimming in! A diving board was for jumping off! And of *course* engineering was messy—but what was wrong with that?

Ellie turned around. The new kids had wandered off, but Kit and Toby were still there. "Why did you tell her we would stop? Can't we ask if they'll move instead?" Ellie asked.

Kit looked disappointed but shrugged. "They were here first. Sometimes it's more important to be nice than to be right. Plus, maybe this will help one of us win Miss Congeniality!"

"What?" Ellie and Toby asked at once.

"It's the award the pageant gives to the person who is the nicest and most helpful. It's a *really* good thing to win, especially because all the other pageant contestants vote on it instead of just the judges. I've won it four times!" Kit said proudly.

"Whoa," Toby said, eyes widening. "So that's the award? Nicest and most helpful?"

"Yep! So maybe you tell another contestant that her ponytail has bumps in it, or help her if she falls down, or ask if someone needs a hug. That sort of thing," Kit explained.

"I can do that!" Toby said, and before Ellie or Kit could say anything, he spun around. "Does anyone here need a hug?" he shouted toward everyone at the pool.

"I don't think he can win, since he isn't in the pageant," Kit whispered to Ellie.

"Well, it doesn't hurt to be nice for no reason," Ellie whispered back, and Kit nodded just as Toby trotted off to see if anyone by the baby pool needed a hug. In the meantime, Ellie turned to look at the diving board, at Melody and her mom, and at the pool. There had to be a way they could finish their cannonball research without bothering Melody!

"Let's think," Ellie said, frowning. "The problem is the splash, so maybe . . . Yes! I've got it!"

Ellie hurried across the pool deck to the lifeguard stand, where a lifeguard was sitting with a red float in his lap.

"Excuse me? Is there a lost and found?" Ellie asked.

"Yep—over there, in the closet by the bathrooms. What did you lose?" the lifeguard asked.

"Nothing! I just need to see if I can borrow what other people have lost!" Ellie said. The lifeguard looked confused, but there was no time to explain—not when there was so much engineering to do.

People were *always* leaving floats at the

pool, especially the ones with holes in them. If there were enough in the lost and found, she could use them to make a splash screen to keep water from hitting Melody and her mom!

Ellie flung open the closet and began to dig through the lost and found. There were coolers and pool noodles and—yes! Floats!

"We aren't going to play with those, are we?" Kit asked from the closet door. "They look like they might have spiders on them."

"We're going to build a splash screen with them!" Ellie explained. "Here, can you hold this?" She handed Kit an alligator-shaped float. Kit took it but held it between her fingers to avoid touching the grimy sitting-in-lost-and-found-for-ages parts. Ellie grabbed all the floats she could find and let the air out of the ones that were still blown up. Then, she and Kit hurried back to the pool deck.

"Whoa, look at that big spider," Toby said when he rejoined them. Kit squealed and threw her float on the ground, even though Toby was pointing to a spider on one of the pool noodles. Ellie shook the spider off into the pine straw and kept moving. She found two closed umbrellas at tables and pulled them out, then she stuck the pool noodle between them and tied it in place with some old whistle lanyards. It was easy after that—just draping the floats across the top.

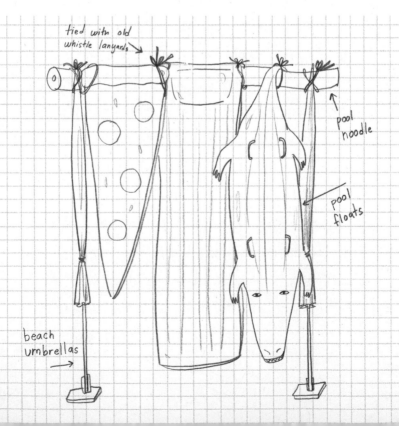

"Now we can take turns holding it up while everyone jumps!" Ellie said. "Go get the other kids—the cannonball experiment is back on!"

Ellie and Toby marched the splash screen across the pool, causing more than a few people to stare—which made sense to Ellie, since it was such a cool idea. They stopped just in front of Melody and her mom, who seemed to have fallen asleep. Perfect! Plus, Ellie figured keeping them from getting woken up by splashes was a great step toward winning that Miss Congeniality award. What was more congenial than keeping someone from getting woken up from a nap?

"This is awesome!" the boy from before said as he raced by her, on the way to the dragon. "I'm going to try the flip again!"

"Okay, but don't land on your head this time! We already know that's a four!" Ellie shouted. The other kids were hurrying over to join in, and Kit was helping them all line up and decide what sort of jumps to do. It was going really well until—

"*Excuse me,*" a voice—a now familiar voice—said.

Ellie cringed, then looked over her shoulder. It was Melody's mom again, with Melody by her side.

"Hi, Melody!" Ellie said, trying to sound like Kit usually did—bright and happy and like a talking piece of cake. "Did you see what we engineered? Now you won't get splashed!"

"And *now* your *thing* is blocking the sun," Melody said, scowling.

"That's probably good," Toby said helpfully. "The sun can be very dangerous. You are wearing sunscreen, aren't you? I read that even if you're wearing sunscreen, you shouldn't sleep in the sun, just in case you sleep for too long and then wake up and are all red like a lobster—"

"I'm wearing sunscreen," Melody said sharply. She scowled, then turned to her mom. "I think Sarah and Betsy are here. Can I find them and take them to play with Pancakes?"

"You're getting pancakes?" Toby asked.

"Pancakes is my rabbit. For my magic act? You've probably seen us in the pageant advertisements," Melody said. Behind the splash screen, someone cannonballed. Ellie bit her lip—she'd missed it! Melody was really wrecking her research. Melody went on. "And if *you* want to be in pageant advertisements—or at least if you want to avoid *embarrassing yourself* in front of the judges—I think you should stop doing whatever this engineering thing is"—she paused to wave at the splash screen— "and start working on being more ladylike."

Ellie just stared for a second, because that was *really* mean, and usually when people were mean, they at least tried to pretend like they weren't being mean. Not Melody, though—in fact, she almost looked pleased with herself!

Kit piped up and even stepped forward a little so that she was almost between Melody and Ellie. "Engineering is perfectly ladylike, Melody, because ladies do it all the time."

Melody turned around and walked away. "Not in pageants they don't!" she called back.

"Bye! I hope Pancakes is doing great! It was wonderful to meet you! Would you like me to get the door? Vote Toby Michaels for Miss Congeniality!" Toby called after them.

Ellie looked at the ground. Toby sure was taking this Miss Congeniality thing seriously, because *she* didn't think it was wonderful to meet Melody Harris at all.

Chapter Five

That night, Ellie and Kit put on their pajamas, which were matching—except that Kit's were pink and Ellie's were purple, and Kit was wearing a pretty necklace and Ellie was wearing her tool belt. They weren't going to sleep—they were going to the Pageant Pajama Party in the hotel lobby! Apparently, there would be popcorn and hot chocolate and a movie to watch.

Ellie didn't really understand why they needed to be in pajamas to do all that, but she decided to just go with it. It was her first pageant, after all, and pageants seemed to do everything a little differently.

"Are those your pajamas?" Ellie asked Toby in the hallway. He was wearing blue pants and a blue shirt and even a blue nightcap, like the kind you saw in storybooks.

"Normally I just wear regular pajamas, but I got these as my special-occasion pajamas," Toby explained, looking very proud. "Good thing I did. I looked up some information on winning Miss Congeniality and read that it's very important to make a good first impression."

They went downstairs together with Kit's mom (who was not wearing pajamas—and was the sort of person who Ellie couldn't imagine wearing something as comfortable as pajamas). The pajama party was already in full swing!

There were plenty of kids Kit and Ellie's age, but there were also some teenage girls and some much younger girls, too—they were competing in the Miss Peachy Keen pageant, too, just not in the same group as Kit and Ellie were. Kit showed Ellie and Toby to the hot chocolate station, where they filled their cups half with marshmallows and half with hot chocolate, then covered the top in peach-colored sprinkles.

"I *extra* love pageants!" Ellie said, looking at her giant mug.

"See? I told you they were fun!" Kit said excitedly. "Come on. I'll introduce you to some of the other contestants! I know almost all of them, since we always compete against one another."

Ellie and Toby followed Kit over to a group of five girls who were sitting in a circle on the floor, eating popcorn. Ellie was sometimes a little scared to walk up to people in circles—sitting in a circle made it look like there was no room for new people, after all—but these girls smiled and waved and opened up right away so that Ellie, Toby, and Kit could sit down.

"Oh, I don't need to sit—can I get anyone another hot cocoa? Another popcorn?" Toby asked the group.

"Um—I guess I would like some more hot cocoa?" a girl with thick black hair twirled on her head said, a little confused.

"Perfect! I'll be right back," he said, then winked at Ellie and Kit as he mouthed, *Miss Congeniality!*

"My name is Piper," the girl with the black hair said, smiling big. "Kit talks about you at pageants all the time! You're an engineer, right?"

Ellie usually said "Yes" right away when someone asked this, but after meeting Melody today, she hesitated. Would these girls be mean to her, too?

"She's a *great* engineer!" Kit said proudly, and that gave Ellie courage.

"I helped Kit with the light-up skateboarding ramp for her talent!" Ellie said.

"A skateboarding ramp! That's so cool," a girl with big blue eyes said. "I juggle for my talent. I wanted to juggle fire this year, but some things happened with the carpet at my dad's house and . . . Well. I'm not going to juggle fire after all."

"Oh!" Ellie said. "I remember you! Emily, right? I saw your picture on the site. I was thinking of a machine I could build to toss you those clubs so your mom doesn't have to! It would be sort of like a robot, and it would be helpful because robots will do the same thing *every* time. With a person, it'll always be a little different." Ellie grabbed her notebook from her tool belt and flipped to the page where she'd drawn the Juggler's Assistant, then showed it to the girl.

Emily was leaning forward, and now her eyes were even bigger. "That's amazing! You'd be able to build that?" she asked in disbelief. The other four girls crowded in to look.

"Not before Sunday," Kit jumped in, giving Ellie a meaningful look. "There won't be enough time, not with the interviews and rehearsals."

"You're probably right," Ellie said with a sigh. "Besides, I still need to add a switch to your skateboard ramp so we can turn the lights on and off easier."

"Do you have time to build something else? I want to see you build something!" Piper said excitedly.

Ellie thought on it for a minute. "Okay—I have an idea. Let's see . . . we need a battery, and some marshmallows, some glue, and some lollipop sticks—or maybe Popsicle sticks. Something sticklike, anyway."

"Lollipop sticks?" one of the girls asked, looking doubtful. "Why do you need lollipop sticks to engineer?"

"You can engineer with lots of things around you—you just have to know how to look!" Ellie said.

"Ooh—I have an idea for something that will work!" Kit said. "I'll be right back!"

Kit dashed off to get whatever her idea was, while a girl named Sarah went for marshmallows, Piper went to find glue, and Ellie hunted for a battery. She found one in the remote control for the big movie projector screen. The movie was only part of the way through, so Ellie figured it couldn't hurt to borrow the battery for a little bit.

Sarah and Piper returned with their supplies (and Toby returned with the hot chocolate

Piper had asked for), and a few moments later, Kit trotted up.

"Will these work?" she asked, giggling a little. She had a red box in her hand; inside were chocolate-covered biscuit sticks, one of her favorite snacks.

"What are those?" Piper asked.

"They're sort of like chocolate cookies," Kit said. "My mom has *her* mom in Japan send them in the mail. They're the best!"

"Ooh, they are," Toby said, munching on one.

"Wait! How many do you need, Ellie?" Kit asked.

"Just two. You can eat the others," Ellie said, and Kit offered them to all the other girls as Ellie got to work. First, she pulled some green-and-red wire bits from her tool belt and wrapped them around the silver ends of the battery. Piper had been able to find only eyelash glue on such short notice, but it worked perfectly for gluing a cookie stick to the bottom and the top of the battery. Ellie ran the wire from the battery up the cookie sticks, and then—

"Hmm . . . we need a super-skinny wire. Something really thin," Ellie said, drumming her pointer finger against her lip. "Wait! I know!" She dashed back through the pajama party and up to the hotel check-in desk, where they had a little cup full of ballpoint pens. Ellie returned, took the pen apart, and pulled out a tiny spring.

"Ooh," Piper said.

"We say that a lot," Toby answered, motioning to himself and Kit. "What are you making anyway?"

Ellie grinned. "A marshmallow slicer!"

With everything hooked up, the pen wire got warmer and warmer until it was downright *hot.* Ellie picked up one of the marshmallows and slid it against the wire. It sliced right through it!

"Whoa—how does it work?" Sarah asked.

"It's all electricity," Ellie explained. She pointed to the battery. "The kind of electricity that makes lights turn on and other stuff like that happen is an electric *current.* It has to go in a circle to work. So the current goes from this end of the battery, through the pen wire, and back into the battery on the other end. The electricity makes the wire hot—but if we had, say, a light or maybe a buzzer, it would make it light up or go *errrrrrrrr.*"

"Wait, but why doesn't the wire over here get hot?" Piper asked, pointing to the pieces attached right to the battery.

"Because there's rubber around it, see? Rubber isn't a good conductor—it's an insulator. That means it doesn't move the current

Marshmallow Cutter

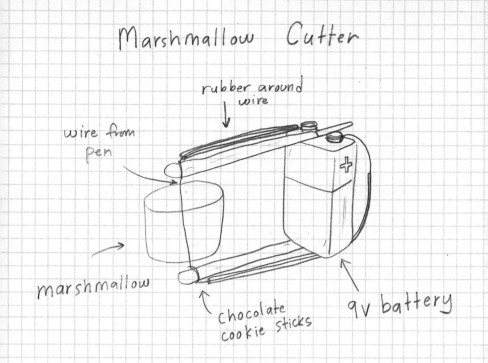

rubber around
wire

wire from
pen

marshmallow

chocolate
cookie sticks

9v battery

very well. Metal is a great conductor, though, so that's why there are wires in all the electrical stuff we use."

"Slice me a piece of marshmallow," Sarah said, holding out her hot chocolate. Ellie sliced everyone pieces of marshmallow for their hot chocolates. She was about to run back for another few marshmallows, since everyone wanted to see it again, when she was stopped by the sound of a door slamming—in fact, *every-thing* at the pajama party seemed to be stopped short by the sound. The room went mostly quiet, except for the movie playing, and people craned their heads to look toward the noise. It didn't take long for whispers of what was going on to reach Ellie and her friends.

"It's Melody Harris! Something's wrong!" a teenage girl near them said.

"Is she okay?" Kit asked.

"Does she need her leg stabilized? Does anyone have a stick I can borrow?" Toby asked, already standing. Kit tugged him back down.

They could just barely see Melody, who was wearing bright-red satin pajamas, making her way across the room and to the stage. The pageant stage was already set up, with lights and backdrops of flowering peach trees. There was a microphone in the middle; Melody walked to it, plucked it off the stand, and then fiddled with the button.

"Testing," she said into the microphone; her voice boomed out across the room. "Hello, friends, parents, fellow Miss Peachy Keen Pageant contestants. Pardon the interruption, but I have a brief announcement."

Melody's voice was tight like a full balloon, and it reminded Ellie of how her teacher talked to her after Ellie had nailed the stapler to the teacher's desk. (Which was really not Ellie's fault, because her teacher had said, *I wish there was a way to keep people from stealing my stapler!* and Ellie had found the perfect way!)

"I'm afraid something terrible has happened," Melody went on. "My rabbit, Pancakes, has been *stolen*."

Chapter Six

The room was full of hissing sounds as everyone at the pajama party began to whisper or gasp or suck air between their teeth in shock at the exact same time. Melody's hands were on her hips; they stayed there as a man from the Miss Peachy Keen Pageant walked up and politely took the microphone away.

"Please, everyone, if you happen to see

Melody's rabbit, let her or a pageant official know immediately. A rabbit can't get very far in a hotel! We'll find this rabbit in no time, Melody."

The man sounded chipper when he said this.

Melody did not look chipper.

Melody looked *furious*. She was good at making *furious* look pretty, but in some ways, that made it even scarier. She walked off the stage, head held high, and joined her mother, who was talking to some of the hotel people and the pageant officials.

"Come on," Kit said, waving for everyone in their little group to stand up. "We should go see how we can help." Ellie could tell that everyone was a little nervous to walk up to Melody, especially when she looked so angry, but they all followed behind Kit.

"Hi, Melody," Kit said as they reached her.

"I'm sorry about Pancakes! Can we help you look?"

"I can organize a search party," Toby said. "We need flashlights, and hats, and a German shepherd—does anyone have a German shepherd?" he asked the other girls.

"I have a wiener dog?" Emily offered.

"That'll work in a pinch," Toby said firmly, nodding.

"I don't need a *search party*," Melody snapped. "Pancakes isn't just *missing*. He was *stolen*."

"Why would anyone steal a rabbit, though?" Ellie asked.

Melody narrowed her eyes. "I know you don't know a lot about pageants, since you're an *engineer*," she said, saying the word in a pretend-high voice, "but obviously someone wanted to sabotage me. Without Pancakes, I can't do my magic act."

All the other pageant contestants looked at one another, shocked. Sabotage? That was ridiculous! Wasn't it? Ellie didn't know enough about pageants to know if sabotage was normal, but based on everyone's faces, she guessed not.

Kit spoke up. "Well, maybe you could borrow Emily's wiener dog until you find Pancakes?"

"I don't think he'll get in a hat," Emily whispered to no one in particular. "He doesn't even like to get in his crate."

Melody didn't hear her, because she was already shouting. "I don't want to pull a wiener dog out of a hat! Magicians pull a *rabbit* out of a hat! And not just any rabbit—Pancakes! It took months and months for him to feel at home in the hat—I can't just replace him with a dog at the last minute! Someone stole my rabbit, and I want him back!"

Kit held her hands up and looked sorrier

than Ellie thought she really needed to look—Melody was the one shouting, after all. "Of course! We'll find Pancakes, Melody. We'll all help look."

Melody took a breath in through her nose that made her nostrils flare up. "I told you: Pancakes isn't *lost*. If we want to find him, I think we should ask all the people who would want to sabotage me. Starting with *you*, Kit."

Kit's eyes widened. Ellie's mouth dropped. The other girls and Toby gasped together in one big breath.

"Melody, I would *never* steal Pancakes!" Kit said.

"Plus, her mom doesn't like inside animals! There's no way she'd let Kit sneak a rabbit into the hotel room," Ellie said. "She wouldn't even let us keep a baby snake in a box on the coffee table last month."

"A *baby snake* isn't the difference between

winning and losing the Miss Junior Peachy Keen title," Melody answered tartly. "Kit was runner-up last year, so I bet she did this to make sure she won this time around!" Melody tilted her chin up and glared, like she was daring Kit to disagree with her.

Even though Ellie knew that Kit *did* disagree with Melody, since this whole sabotage thing was just ridiculous, Kit wasn't the sort of girl who got glared at very often—which meant Kit didn't quite know what to do. Ellie grabbed hold of Kit's hand, because all the glaring might very well make Kit cry right here in front of everyone. (Which Ellie knew she would be embarrassed about, even though Ellie felt like being accused of rabbit stealing was a perfectly fine reason to cry.)

"Come on, Kit," Ellie said. "We all know you didn't take Pancakes. Let's go back to the hot chocolate bar."

Kit let Ellie tug her away, but Ellie could tell she really wanted to stay and convince Melody she hadn't taken Pancakes. Kit couldn't stand it when someone was angry with her! Ellie was pretty sure there was no convincing Melody, though—at least not right now.

"She's just upset," Ellie said as they reached the hot chocolate bar. "Sometimes people say things they don't mean when they're upset. It's no excuse, but it happens all the same."

Toby, who had walked along behind them, nodded. "And besides, Kit—everyone knows you're no rabbit thief."

"Everyone but Melody," Kit said sadly. "What do you think *really* happened to Pancakes? I can't imagine anyone stealing a rabbit."

Ellie shrugged. "Maybe he's just lost. Rabbits are clever. They get under garden fences, so I bet they can sneak out of cage fences."

Toby was in the middle of tidying up the

hot chocolate bar by sweeping crumbs to the floor and replacing spilled candies in their dishes. He ate a few instead of putting them back. "You should try doing what my baseball coach says."

"Those flowers are for seeing not picking?" Ellie asked, because that was what her tee-ball coach always said back before she realized she didn't really like tee-ball.

"No—he says to *keep your eyes on the prize! Don't get distracted! Stop scratching your butt!*" Toby said, making his voice rough and loud.

"I don't think I understand," Kit said politely.

Toby ate a few more pieces of candy. "You didn't take Melody's rabbit, so all you can do is keep your eyes on the prize—the pageant. *I'm* keeping my eyes on the Miss Congeniality award."

"*And* you're not scratching your butt!" Ellie said, giving him a thumbs-up.

"See? We're all doing great! Don't worry about Melody," Toby said, shaking his head in Melody's direction.

But even though Kit nodded and got a new hot chocolate (this time with peanut butter candies in it), Ellie could tell that her best friend was very, *very* worried about Melody.

Chapter Seven

It was Saturday, the first real day of the Miss Peachy Keen Pageant! It was mostly *good* exciting, but almost everyone was talking about Pancakes, which made it a tiny bit *bad* exciting. Still, Ellie was going to get to wear high heels for the first time in her life! They weren't really *that* high, but they were purple and sparkly, and Ellie felt like she looked extremely fancy when she wore them, especially since they were the exact same color as the flowers she'd drawn on her electric drill.

Today, all the pageant contestants were practicing how they'd walk out and say their names in the microphone. It sounded pretty easy, until Ellie learned they had to walk out in a certain way, and then go line up in a certain spot, and then stand in a certain position, all of which left Ellie feeling very *un*certain. Ellie was glad she'd worn her tool belt—wearing her tool belt always made her feel better about doing something new.

"You'll be great!" Kit promised as they stood backstage. Kit tapped on her chest to remind Ellie that they were wearing matching necklaces—Japanese coins that had square holes right through them, which were perfect for putting on a string. Kit's mom said they were good luck, so Kit always wore one to pageants. Kit was great at pageants, so Ellie figured they really must be lucky.

Backstage at the pageant wasn't quite like it was when her class did a Thanksgiving play in the high school's theater—this wasn't a theater, after all; it was a hotel. There were big curtains set up to keep people in the audience from seeing the contestants, but it was still bright, and there were no curtain ropes or fat cables to trip over in the dark (which Ellie preferred, since she'd fallen down and ripped the arm of her mashed potatoes costume the night of the play). All the pageant contestants were in a big long line, from the littlest girls to the oldest ones. Ellie's group was right in the middle, with Piper walking out first and Melody Harris walking out last. Melody was wearing her Miss Junior Peachy Keen crown—she had won the pageant last year.

"Just remember to put your hand on your hip," Piper told Ellie helpfully as they waited.

"And smile!" Sarah added.

"And look up," Emily added. "Don't look at the ground!"

Melody snorted. Ellie turned to look and saw that Melody was staring right at Kit and her, and even though Ellie didn't speak *snort*, she was pretty sure that snort meant something not very nice about the two of them.

"She's right," Melody said, which made both Ellie and Kit raise their eyebrows high. Melody kept going. "Don't worry about me. Worry about that weird engineering belt you're wearing. The judges aren't going to give high points to a girl who *accessorizes* with a hammer." Then she giggled really loudly—loudly enough that some of the girls nearby her started to giggle, too, even though they didn't seem to think it was especially funny.

Kit tilted her chin up, looking brave, and grabbed Ellie's hand. It wasn't until she did this that Ellie realized just how mean Melody was being—somehow, up until Kit got upset, Ellie was more confused than anything else.

After all, why would the judges think her tool belt was an accessory, like earrings or a bracelet? It was obviously a *tool belt*. It was for tools not prettiness.

But Kit being upset made Ellie realize she was being made fun of, which made her face grow hot and her tool belt feel especially heavy. Kit turned around and tugged on Ellie's hand until she turned around, too.

"Should I take it off?" Ellie asked Kit quietly.

Kit squeezed her hand tighter and gave Ellie a really serious look. "No! You wanted to wear it, and so you should. Besides, I think the way the hammer clinks on that little metal part makes a pretty noise, like you're carrying a teeny bell. You'll sound like a fairy princess when you walk out!"

Kit always knew just what to say.

Of course, fairy princesses probably didn't

wobble when they wore high heels. Ellie looked down at her feet. Even though these were the prettiest shoes she'd ever owned, they were way harder to walk in than her sneakers or her sandals. Every time she took a step, she wobbled back and forth like she was on a balance beam.

There were still a few minutes to go until all the girls her age went out—just enough time for a super-quick fix. Ellie slid off her shoes and looked at them closely, thinking hard.

"What are you doing?" Kit whispered.

"Is she taking off her shoes? Ew! That's so *unsanitary*!" Melody said from the back of the line. Ellie ignored her—which was a little easier to do now that her brain was too full of engineering thoughts to let Melody thoughts squish in.

Ellie had been taking ballet classes for a whole year and a half, so she knew it was easier to balance on your whole foot than it was to balance on your tippy-toes. Wearing high heels meant she *had* to stand on her tiptoes, though, so that couldn't be helped. But . . .

"Standing on something that's wide is easier than standing on something that's skinny," Ellie said thoughtfully. "So I just need . . . Hmm . . ." Ellie looked around. There wasn't

tin-can stilts

chip-can stilts

wide base = easy to walk on

thin base = harder to walk on

very much backstage to work with—but she knew where she could find what she needed.

"I'll be right back!" Ellie whispered to Kit, and then left her shoes and crawled out under the curtain.

A few people in the audience gave her confused looks as she appeared, but most of them went back to watching the girls who were already walking out onstage. Ellie waved to her mom, who waved back; Kit's mom was sitting with her and looked very concerned, but Ellie's mom just shrugged. She was used to Ellie running off to build something, after all.

At the back of the room was the big table where they'd checked in the day before—the one with all the candy and flowers and confetti. Ellie looked at the table, then saw what she needed—the cardboard heart cutouts that the candy dishes were sitting on. She grabbed two of them, then went to the pageant bulletin board. There were lots of little notices about dresses for sale and flyers about fancy makeup and official-looking forms and, thankfully, a whole line of unused pushpins down at the bottom. Ellie grabbed a few—

There was a noise from the stage, and Ellie turned. A pageant person was on it, announcing that the contestants from the Miss Junior Peachy Keen division were up next! Ellie yelped and sprinted back to the curtain. She dove underneath it like a softball player sliding for a base, smacking into the ankles of some of the teenage girls.

"Sorry, sorry! I'm trying to walk in my high heels!" Ellie said, then darted back to her place in line. Piper was already walking out! There wasn't very much time. Kit was going out now, and Sarah—

Ellie grabbed her hammer from her tool belt, then flipped her high heels over. She lined the cardboard hearts up against the heel, then very carefully tap-tap-tapped the pushpin through the cardboard hearts and into the bottom of the heel. Then she did the same with the other shoe. She heard some of the contestants talking—Melody, she could tell, was talking about her—and worked really hard not to listen to it.

"Contestant number eight, Miss Ellie Bell!" the pageant lady said in a very announcer-y voice. Ellie scrambled to her feet—this was one

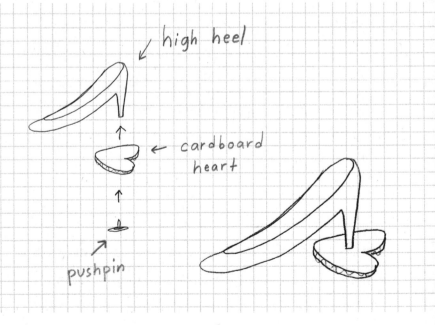

high heel

← cardboard heart

pushpin

build that wouldn't get much testing before it had to work. She took one step, then another, then another—

"Here she is, Miss Ellie—erm—" the pageant lady said as Ellie stepped up onto the stage. Ellie smiled big and walked to the front of the stage like she was supposed to. She put her hand on her hip and waved. And she did it *all* without wobbling. The high heel balancers worked!

"Miss Ellie Bell!" the pageant lady said, giving the judges a shrug and a grin. Ellie turned and walked back toward the line of girls and saw Kit grinning at her. She stood in the line with the other contestants while the last few girls from her group walked up, waved, and went to stand in line. Melody was the last one. Ellie noticed she had *very* tall heels on, and just like Kit, she didn't wobble at all, even without high heel balancers.

"Wonderful, everyone!" the pageant lady said

when they were finished. "Now remember—everyone has their interview this afternoon. Don't be late! Parents, check your schedules to help remind your future Miss Junior Peachy Keen!" She said this last part out at the audience, and bunches of parents nodded back. Then she added, "Also, just a reminder that our reigning Miss Junior Peachy Keen is still missing her rabbit, Pancakes. Please keep an eye out! He could still be in the hotel!"

And just like that, all of Ellie's excitement over walking in her fancy shoes was smashed to the ground—because now, all she could think about was how the very same girl who had made fun of her tool belt was calling Kit a rabbit thief. Ellie couldn't help but wonder two things: first, how could someone be so mean? And second, what would Melody Harris do next?

Chapter Eight

That afternoon, Ellie, Kit, Toby, and Piper were waiting outside one of the hotel's big meeting rooms. It was the kind with a long table down the middle and chairs that rolled *and* spun—although the people in the meeting room weren't doing either of those things (which seemed like a real waste to Ellie). They were the judges, and it was the interview part of the pageant—where they talked to each contestant. Ellie was up next, then Piper, then Kit; Toby, meanwhile, was being extra congenial by helping everyone prepare for their interview, offering to let them practice their handshakes with him.

"I read on the Internet that you want to make sure your hand doesn't feel like a dead fish," Toby explained then shook Kit's hand again.

"I've never touched a dead fish, so I'm not sure what that feels like," Kit said, frowning.

"I think slimy," Toby said thoughtfully. "Though maybe dry? The Internet didn't say if it was a fish that was dead in the water or one that was dead in the grocery store."

Kit looked like all this dead-fish talk was making her feel a little sick. She took her hand from Toby and gave him a weak smile. "I think I've got it now. Thanks."

"No problem! Piper, do you want to practice?

Remember: make eye contact! And tell them you're goal-oriented. That was on lots of the websites."

"I think that's for a different sort of interview," Piper said, but she started shaking Toby's hand anyhow.

"Are you nervous?" Kit asked Ellie.

"Not really," Ellie said, shrugging. "Especially since I get to wear sneakers now."

Kit smiled. She was wearing sneakers, too, although hers were very clean, whereas Ellie's had lots of grass stains. They both had on fluffy skirts and the Miss Peachy Keen Pageant T-shirt, and even though Kit's mom had thought it was a *very* bad idea, Ellie was wearing her tool belt again. Kit's mom thought lots of things Ellie liked were *very* bad ideas, so Ellie didn't take it all that personally.

Kit looked like she was just about to say something else to Ellie when she suddenly bit her lip and looked down at her hands.

"*Ahem,*" a voice said over Ellie's shoulder. Ellie spun around—it was Melody Harris, standing up very straight and still wearing her shiny silver Miss Junior Peachy Keen crown.

"Hello," Ellie said to Melody, because she wasn't really sure what you were supposed to say back to "ahem." She noticed that Melody had a stack of orange papers in her arms. "What are those?" Ellie asked.

Melody smiled, but it wasn't an especially nice smile. "Here," she said, and passed a piece of paper to Ellie. Quick as a flash, she passed papers to Kit, Toby, and Piper, too. Ellie's heart sank—it was a flyer. There was a photo of Pancakes on it, just under the word "stolen." The worst part, though, was that underneath the photo was a drawing of a stick-figure person stealing a stick-figure rabbit. And the stick-figure person? It looked an awful lot like Kit.

"You can just call or text this number if you happen to find Pancakes," Melody said, holding up the flyer and pointing to the phone number at the bottom. "In the meantime, I've been practicing my gymnastics routine for my backup talent, and it's very *high point* quality, if you ask me. So whoever *stole* him might as well return him, since it isn't going to change who wins this year's crown."

"I really hope you find him, Melody," Kit said in a very tiny voice. Ellie grabbed Kit's hand and squeezed it, but it didn't seem to help. Ellie was about to say something to Melody—to tell her that she didn't need to be so mean, or that she shouldn't say people are thieves if she didn't know for sure, or to tell her that maybe rabbits don't like being in hats anyway.

Before she could say any of that, though, Toby said, "Would anyone like a mint?"

Everyone turned to him.

"Huh?" Melody asked, then, looking startled, changed it to, "Pardon?"

"A mint. I got a roll for fifty cents at the hotel store," he said, pulling a tube of mint candy from his pocket. "I read that having fresh breath is *very* important at an interview."

"I'll take one!" Piper said eagerly, though Ellie suspected it was mostly to get everyone's attention *completely* off Melody and her flyers.

"Me too," Kit said weakly. Ellie shrugged and popped a mint into her mouth; Melody rolled her eyes.

"Good luck in your interviews, girls," Melody said, even though it didn't sound like she meant it. She then gave Ellie a wary look. "I see you're wearing that weird belt again. At least from the stage it didn't seem so . . . grimy."

Ellie tried to look like this didn't bother her and shrugged extra big. "Well, of course it's grimy. It's a tool belt. They get grimy when you're building things all the time."

Melody made a face. "Building things? *All* the time? Don't you ever do anything fun?"

"Building things is a lot of fun," Ellie said, but her voice was a teeny bit smaller.

"It's true! I love helping Ellie build things," Kit said, looking over at Toby, who nodded.

"It's pretty great. There was the time we broke a bunch of pickle jars, which wasn't so great, but I don't much like pickles anyhow."

Now Melody made an even facier face. "Right. Well, I guess I shouldn't be surprised that a rabbit thief would have such *weirdo* friends," she said in a sort of singsong voice, then turned and started down the hallway. "Good luck in there, Ellie! I hope the judges don't notice your tool belt smells so pickle-y!" she called back.

"Wait!" Toby called after Melody. "Would

you like to practice your handshake before you go? That's the *most* important part of the interview! Vote Toby for Miss Congeniality!" Melody didn't look back again. "I guess I can't count on her vote," he said with a sigh.

"Probably not," Ellie said. She unclipped her tool belt and handed it to Kit—

"It *doesn't* smell like pickles," Kit told her firmly. "At least, not anymore. We got most of the juice out, remember?"

"I know—but she's probably right about it being a little grimy, don't you think? I don't want to be bad at pageants because I didn't listen," Ellie answered, trying not to sound as sad as she felt. She hated taking off her tool belt! But even if she was mean, Melody was still last year's pageant winner. She probably knew best, right? And it wasn't like Ellie had seen a single other contestant wearing a tool belt . . .

The door to the meeting room opened,

and Emily, who had been doing her interview, walked out. She was smiling but looked relieved that the interview was over. One of the pageant people leaned through the door. Ellie couldn't really tell if it was the same pageant lady who had helped on the stage earlier—all the grown-ups here looked an awful lot alike, if you asked her. "Miss Ellie Bell? You're up!" the lady said.

"Remember—don't have dead fish for hands!" Toby whispered as Ellie started toward the door.

Ellie accidentally thought about someone with dead fish for hands, which would have made her laugh—except all she could think about was how her waist felt really strange without her tool belt wrapped snugly around it. There was no clink from her hammer; there was no jangle of the screws and nails in the front pocket. Ellie didn't feel like an engineer—in fact, she didn't even feel like *Ellie*. But maybe that was a good thing? Ellie, after all, had never competed in a pageant. Maybe Not Ellie would be better at it than Ellie was.

She stepped into the meeting room, and suddenly, Ellie understood why Kit said lots of people were nervous about the interview. The room was very quiet, and there were three people sitting at the end of the table, one man and two ladies. They were wearing very nice clothes, the sort that you could wear only if you knew you could sit very still, and they had very smooth skin. Ellie had never really noticed if someone's skin was smooth before, but theirs was *so* smooth that it was impossible not to.

"Hello, Miss Bell!" the man said, smiling. He reached out his hand, and Ellie knew just what to do—she shook it, then shook the two ladies' hands, and she felt pretty good about it not being at all like holding a dead fish.

"Have a seat," the lady who had come to the

door said, so Ellie did. "Now, Miss Bell, we're just going to talk to you for a minute. Remember that there are no wrong answers, okay? Just be yourself."

"Really?" Ellie asked.

"Of course! We want to know who you really are," the lady said cheerfully.

Ellie pressed her lips together, then scooched up into the seat. She swung her legs back and forth nervously. Did they *really* want her to be herself? Engineering and grimy tool belt and all? It was hard to know for sure.

They asked Ellie about her favorite class at school (art) and her best friend (Kit). They wanted to know what her favorite color was (purple then pink) and if she had any pets (no, but Kit had a pet sheep named Penelope that sometimes played in her backyard, so it was kind of like having a pet). An interviewer was about to ask something else when suddenly, there was a loud *whooooosh*, and all the lights in the room went out at once.

"Ugh," one of the ladies said. "They blew the power again!"

"It's the Miss girls. They're all turning on their hair dryers at once, and I guess it just kills the whole floor," the man said, shaking his head. He looked to Ellie. "Don't worry— they'll have it back on in no time. I don't know why hair dryers make this happen. It's just hot air!"

"Oh!" Ellie said.

The interviewers looked at her. Ellie mashed her lips together. She knew *exactly* why hair dryers made this happen! But all she could think about was Melody and the mean things she'd said.

"Are you all right? It isn't too dark in here with the windows!" one of the ladies said helpfully, like she thought perhaps Ellie was afraid of the dark.

"It's because of the current," Ellie said quickly, then smashed her lips back together.

"I'm sorry?" the man asked.

Ellie sighed. There was no use. She couldn't not talk about engineering, not when engineering was right in her face like this. She took a breath and explained. "Hair dryers need a *lot* of power. More than a regular light bulb. If you turn on too many at once, they're asking for more power than the wire can give them."

"Oh! So it all shuts down?" a woman said, looking so interested that it gave Ellie hope—maybe she *wasn't* embarrassing herself!

"Yes! And it does that on purpose. If you have too much current going through wire, it can get hot and cause a fire. So when there's too much current, there's a circuit breaker that steps in and says *stop*. I mean, it doesn't actually say that—but it steps in and breaks the circuit, so the current stops traveling. That

way nothing burns down, but it makes everything on the circuit stop working."

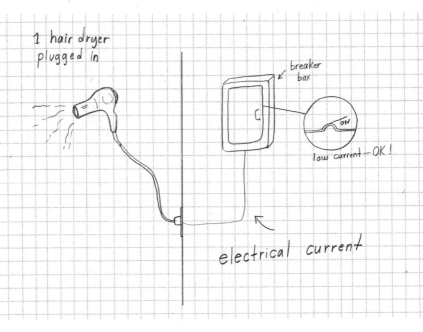

1 hair dryer
plugged in

breaker
box

ON

low current — OK!

electrical current

"Like the lights," one of the ladies said,
motioning toward the ceiling.

"Yep. So someone will just need to go and
fix the circuit breaker, and then everything
will come back on again. Or at least, it'll come
back on until they turn on all the hair dryers
at once."

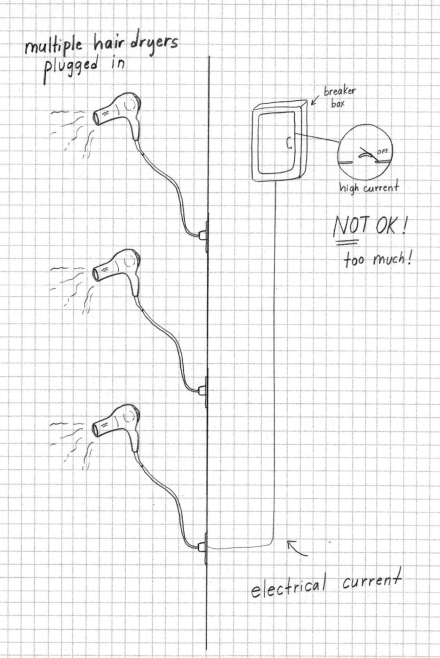

multiple hair dryers
plugged in

breaker
box

OFF

high current

NOT OK!
too much!

electrical current

"Which they apparently keep doing," the man said, shaking his head. "This is the fourth time this morning!"

Just as he said this, the lights came back on, and everyone in the room gave a little cheer. One of the pageant ladies smiled at Ellie. "How did you know about that?" she asked.

"I'm an engineer," Ellie explained, feeling better about this now that the judges seemed so impressed.

"An engineer!" one of the ladies said. "That sounds like so much fun! What, exactly, do you engineer?"

"All sorts of things! Sometimes things for friends, like hair braiders or water-balloon launchers or elevators or skate ramps or sheep houses," Ellie said.

"Goodness," the man said. "It sounds like you're very helpful."

Ellie nodded. "That's what engineering is—you find or make or build ways to help people."

One of the pageant people laughed a little and looked over at the other grown-ups. "I can think of a good way to help—engineer a way to find that lost rabbit before Mrs. Harris calls her lawyer!"

Ellie's eyes went wide.

"I'm just joking, dear—don't worry," the lady said quickly.

Ellie knew she was joking, though—that wasn't the point. The point was . . . the lady was *right*. Not about the lawyer—well, maybe about the lawyer, but Ellie didn't know anything about that—but about finding Pancakes.

"So if I engineered something to catch Pancakes . . . that wouldn't be embarrassing?" Ellie asked carefully.

The pageant judges looked a little confused,

but then the lady who'd made the joke about the lawyer leaned forward. "You should never be embarrassed about helping someone, Miss Bell."

Ellie bit her lip but then grinned. "Can I just borrow one of those sheets of paper real quick? And a pen?"

"Er, sure," the man said, and pulled a piece of paper from his clipboard. He passed it, along with a pen, to her. Ellie pressed the paper as flat as she could on her leg and began to draw.

"What are you doing?" the man asked.

"I'm engineering," she said seriously.

Chapter Nine

PROJECT NUMBER 82: RABBIT CATCHER

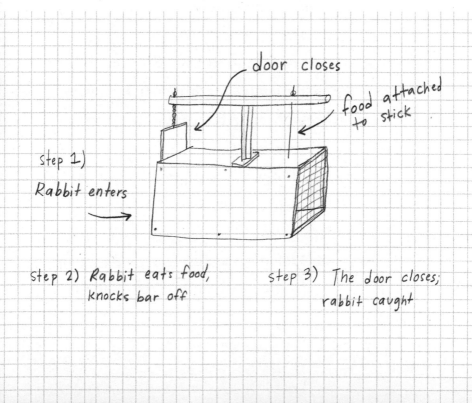

door closes

food attached
to stick

step 1)
Rabbit enters

step 2) Rabbit eats food,
knocks bar off

step 3) The door closes;
rabbit caught

"If Pancakes is still in the hotel, this will catch him," Ellie said, showing Toby her plans while Kit was in her interview. Toby's eyes got big as he looked at the drawing.

"What if he's not in the hotel at all, though?" Toby asked.

Ellie frowned. "Well, then this won't catch him—but I think it's our best chance all the same. Besides, I don't think he could have gotten very far without being seen. I say he's still here somewhere, just hiding."

"Rabbits are prey animals, so they *would* hide," Toby said thoughtfully. "So are squirrels. Well, technically, anything can be a prey animal if something is hunting it, but rabbits are more prey animal than—"

"Let's look for building supplies!" Ellie said before Toby could get too carried away.

"Wait," Toby said, stopping her. "I don't understand. Melody is being so mean to you and Kit! And I guess to me, too, but she just called me a 'weirdo,' which I don't think is a bad thing, honestly. But why do you want to help her?"

Ellie took a breath. "Because that's what engineers do—they help people. All people. Even people who are mean. I'm an engineer, and Melody isn't going to change that, no matter how much she makes fun of it! And besides—if we catch Pancakes, we prove that Kit isn't the rabbit thief at all."

Toby smashed his lips all to one side of his face, like he wasn't convinced. "I guess . . ."

"Well, it would also be very *congenial* if we helped her."

Toby's face went back to normal. "You're definitely right about *that*. Let's start looking."

They hurried through the hotel, eyes peeled for anything that might work. Some parts were easy—they could use a pencil for the trip trigger, and one of the older pageant contestants gave them a hair ribbon for the string bit. They caught Emily in the hallway, and she went to the prop storage place, where Kit's skate ramp was, to get them one of her practice twirling batons for the bar on top. That left only the main part of the trap. Finding a box that was big enough to hold a rabbit but strong enough to *contain* a rabbit was tricky.

"What about one of those long skinny soda boxes?" Toby wondered as they stood in the hotel ballroom. The oldest pageant contestants were practicing their entrances now, and they were really, really good at walking in high heels. Ellie wondered if they'd practiced a lot or if that was just one of those things you understood how to do when you got older, like making spaghetti or the way credit cards worked.

"That would work if Pancakes was a really small rabbit, I guess, but he looks pretty big on the flyer," Ellie said, motioning to one of Melody's bright-orange "Stolen" flyers. They were everywhere—on the walls, on pillars, on each and every step going up to the second floor of the hotel restaurant, in stacks on end tables—

"Oh!" Ellie said. "The end tables!"

"They're nice, I guess, if you like modern design," Toby said, frowning.

"No, no—they're the perfect shape!" Ellie said. The end tables were tall and skinny—which means that on their sides, they were long and narrow. They didn't have sides, of course, so they weren't really a box . . . but finding something to make box sides out of wouldn't be that hard!

"I don't know that we're allowed to build with the furniture, though," Toby said.

"I bet we are if someone asks *extra* nicely," Ellie said. "Like, if someone were to be *extra* congenial?"

Toby grinned. He had always been very good at talking to grown-ups, even *before* he wanted to be Miss Congeniality, so this would be easy-peasy. Ellie sat on one of the lobby couches while Toby walked over to the front desk, head held high and arms swinging at his sides. He looked very official, walking like that. The people at the front desk smiled down at him, and Toby began to speak. He waved his hands a lot, gestured to one of the end tables, laughed, then reached forward and shook the front desk person's hand.

"We can borrow one! But I had to *negotiate*, and I promised we wouldn't put any nail holes in it," Toby said, grinning.

"You're the best!" Ellie said, bouncing on her heels. "What did you say?"

"Oh, this and that," Toby said, shrugging proudly. "You know how it is. You talk a little about their kids, ask about the weather, and then ask to borrow an end table to make a rabbit trap."

Ellie didn't know at all how that was but nodded anyway. They picked up one of the end tables and carried it up to Ellie's hotel room, where her mom was sitting on the bed, watching movies as she sewed lots of little beaded hearts onto the hem of Ellie's big fluffy ball gown.

"What's all that?" Ellie's mom asked. "Isn't that a table from the lobby?"

"A build! And we have permission for the table," Ellie said excitedly, and pulled her hammer from her tool belt. "We're making a rabbit trap to catch Pancakes!"

"Shouldn't a rabbit trap catch *rabbits*?" Ellie's mom asked, but Ellie could tell by the way she was smirking that she knew very well that Pancakes was the name of a rabbit and not just a breakfast food. "Well, if you're going to be hammering in here, I'm going to go visit with Toby's mom for a while." She started toward the door; Toby rushed back to it and opened it for her, bowing a little as she walked through, looking confused.

"Remember—vote Toby for Miss Congeniality!" he said as she disappeared down the hallway.

"I don't think she gets to vote," Ellie said.

Toby shrugged. "Well, maybe she'll tell her friends."

Ellie suspected that her mom's friends wouldn't get to vote, either, but focused on the build instead.

They were just finishing up when there was a knock on the door, quiet and quick—it was Kit, Ellie knew, even before Toby rushed to open the door for her.

"Where did you guys go? I came out of my interview and couldn't find you anywhere!" she said. "And did you see the lobby? Melody put those awful posters up everywhere. Orange, orange, orange on every single wall."

"We did—and we have a solution," Ellie said proudly, motioning to the rabbit catcher.

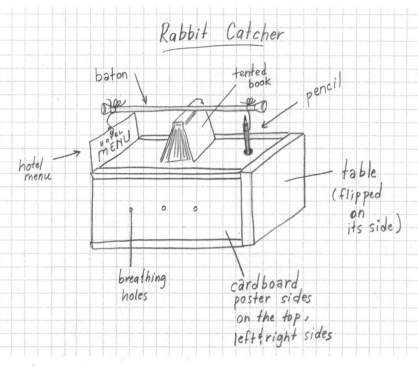

Rabbit Catcher

baton

tented book

pencil

hotel menu

HOTEL MENU

table (flipped on its side)

breathing holes

cardboard poster sides on the top, left & right sides

Kit's eyes brightened, but then her smile went a little sideways. "Wait. What is it?"

"A rabbit catcher," Ellie said. "Don't worry, Kit—we're going to find Pancakes and prove you're no rabbit thief."

Chapter Ten

Ellie, Kit, and Toby spent the rest of the afternoon checking and double-checking the rabbit
catcher. They drew stars on the sides and a sign
that said Pancakes, Come Here on the door, just
in case Pancakes was like those animals you
see on the news who know how to read or say
"hello." At five o'clock, Ellie's mom returned,
with Kit's and Toby's moms behind her.

"Time for dinner!" she said. "Are you three finished with your build?"

"Yep! Now we just need to set it up," Ellie said, pleased. She slid on her flip-flops then lifted the rabbit trap up with Kit's and Toby's help.

"Where are you going to put it?" Toby asked eagerly. "Outside Melody's room? By the front doors?"

"I don't think the people who run the hotel would be pleased about that by the front door," Kit's mom said a little warily. "And wait—isn't that one of the tables from the lobby?"

"I imagine you'd want to put it near a food source," Toby's mom said thoughtfully. "That's where we had to put a trap to catch a raccoon once."

"By your fridge?" Ellie asked.

Toby's mom wrinkled her nose. "No. By the trash cans. Raccoons don't much care if the food is fresh."

Toby nodded in agreement. "They also don't much care about where they go to the bathroom, and so if you have raccoons, your dad should *not* walk to get the newspaper barefoot because he'll step—"

"I think they get the idea," Toby's mom broke in, though it looked like now she couldn't stop thinking about the stuff raccoons left for people to step in.

The six of them got a table in the hotel dining room, and after they ordered their food, Ellie grabbed a handful of carrots from the salad bar. She ate a few loudly so her mom would know that she'd done it, and then tucked the rest into the back of the rabbit trap. Now she just needed to find a rabbit food source, like Toby's mom had suggested. The salad bar looked like a *perfect* rabbit food source, but Ellie knew they'd take the veggies away after dinner was over. The *real* food source would be wherever the veggies went next.

Ellie looked over at her mom, but she was in the middle of a conversation with the other two moms, and there was nothing worse than trying to break into a Mom Conversation. "I'll be right back. Don't eat all my chicken nuggets!" she said out loud, aiming the last comment at Toby.

"What? That was one time! And you looked finished!" Toby called after her.

Ellie carried the rabbit trap across the dining room then pushed through the kitchen door. She knew that she was probably not *supposed* to be in the kitchen, but it wasn't like she was just poking around for fun. This was important engineer business! It smelled like soap, and there were lots of people in uniforms, and the whole place was steamy from the dishwasher hissing on the far end. She took a step—

Everyone stopped working to look at her.

"Are you looking for the bathroom? This

isn't the right spot. Here, I'll show you—" a server said, and took a step toward Ellie.

"Oh, no," Ellie said quickly. "I'm not lost. I just needed to place this rabbit catcher by wherever you throw away leftover vegetables, since that'll be a rabbit food source."

The server looked confused, like she was replaying Ellie's words again in her head to make sure she'd heard them right. "What?"

"I'm trying to catch an escaped rabbit. Pancakes? Perhaps you've seen the flyers?"

"Oh!" the server said, eyes widening. "*That* rabbit! I thought he was stolen!"

"It's really hard to say what happened," Ellie said, forcing a smile. "But can I set my trap for him, just in case?"

"Um . . ." The server looked over to some of the other kitchen workers, who shrugged. "Okay," the server answered. "Follow me. Don't slip!"

Ellie followed the server toward the back of

the kitchen, past some giant silver freezers and an ice machine, until they finally came to a trash bin.

"This is the compost trash—all the leftover veggies go in here. Who made the trap for you?" the server asked as Ellie stooped to set it up by the edge of the bin.

"I did! I'm an engineer," Ellie explained.

"*You* made it? You didn't just do the decorations?" the server asked, impressed.

"Yep," Ellie said. "I make lots of things. I made a skate ramp with lights on it for my friend Kit—she's going to be skateboarding on it in the pageant tomorrow."

"With lights? Wow," the server said. Then she added, "She made that! And lights on a skate ramp!" Ellie looked up to see that two other restaurant people had come to watch what was going on. Ellie smiled and got the trap set up, then she showed them how it worked.

"That's really clever! Can you engineer

something else?" a man in a white chef's jacket asked.

"Sure! Maybe . . ." Ellie looked around. It was a very tidy kitchen, and whoever kept things in shape was doing a good job—it didn't even look like there was a wobbly table to level! She saw a little clock timer on a counter and got an idea—

"Can I borrow that?" she asked. "And then I need a lemon. I'll give it back, I promise!"

The chef shrugged then nabbed the clock timer from the counter and a few lemons from a clear bin packed full of them.

"I just need the one. I can make it into a battery. Watch!" Ellie said. She took the lemon then fished in her tool belt for a nail and some of the wire she'd been using on Kit's skateboard ramp lights. She poked the nail into the lemon and then stabbed the wire into it on the opposite end. A few more grown-ups

gathered around, and Ellie got just a little bit
nervous. Sometimes builds went wrong, after
all—but she'd done this one before, and it was
usually easy-peasy.

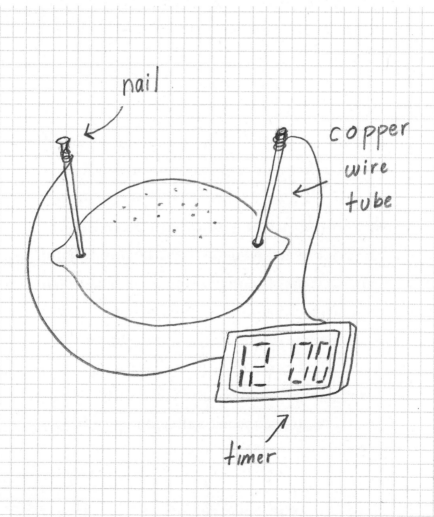

"It works because the lemon and the wire and the nail all make the circuit into a circle. So if I just touch the wire to the metal bits where the battery goes . . . ," Ellie said as she pulled the battery door off the back of the little clock. Then she poked the wire at the metal bits inside the clock battery area.

"Whoa! It's on! It's really working!" one of the cooks said, pointing. He was right—the clock was on! The crowd around her seemed impressed—a few clapped. Ellie beamed.

"A lemon isn't *really* a battery, exactly, but it works because the sour part of the lemon— the acid—*reacts* to the metal in the wire and the nail, so it makes a teeny-tiny bit of electricity. Just enough to make the clock turn on."

"That's a real talent you have there!" one said.

"Thanks," Ellie said, then added a little sadly, "but don't worry—I'm doing ballet in the pageant. Engineering isn't really for pageants."

The server tilted her head to the side and looked like she might ask but then decided against it. Ellie returned the clock and the lemon, which had two little holes in it, like a lemon-vampire had sucked on it. She stepped back out into the dining room, which was a lot quieter and drier than the kitchen, and started toward her table when she stopped suddenly.

Walking into the dining room was Melody Harris.

Chapter Eleven

Melody was, of course, wearing her crown, along with a very nice dress that had no wrinkles at all in it, not even where dresses always wrinkle in your lap after sitting. She was standing beside her mom, who was wearing a matching dress, and Ellie thought it was pretty amazing that *two* people could stay so unwrinkled. She was just wondering if there was a way to learn how to stay unwrinkled (that seemed like a useful skill to have) when Melody spotted her and, to Ellie's surprise, walked over.

"Hi, Melody," Ellie said.

"Ellie," Melody said, putting her hands on her hips. "Is it true you built a *contraption* to catch Pancakes?"

Ellie's eyebrows went way, way up. "Yes! But how did you find out? I only just—"

"The interviewers told me you drew it right there in your interview!" Melody said. "Which, by the way, is *not* what you're supposed to do in an interview. I don't want any of your engineering around my rabbit, Ellie. It's weird, and I don't want people to think I *approve*."

"Hi, Melody!" Kit said in a hopeful voice, walking up behind her. Toby was on his way but had been held back by folding his napkin neatly and putting it on his chair.

"Kit," Melody said as if she'd just smelled something gross. "I assume you already know about the *contraption* Ellie built to catch Pancakes?"

"Yes! It's really cool, Melody. I think it'll work perfectly," Kit said, nodding enthusiastically.

"I was just telling Ellie that I don't approve of it," Melody said, tilting her nose up. When neither Ellie nor Kit responded to this, Melody sighed dramatically. "I guess it's fine if you want to leave it set, Ellie, since you already *engineered* it or whatever. But if it *does* work—which it won't—then it better not hurt him. He's a very rare breed of rabbit, you know."

Ellie paused then said—slowly, because she wasn't sure she really wanted to say it—"Do you want to see the rabbit trap, Melody? It's just through there, by the trash bins." She motioned toward the kitchen doors.

Melody bit her lip then craned her neck around Ellie and stared at the doors for a few seconds. "Pancakes would *never* play around trash bins. He's a very clean rabbit."

"Of course. We thought that maybe he'd also be a very *hungry* rabbit," Ellie said. "I'm sure he's very clean normally."

"Well, and he's also very tired, I'm sure," Melody went on. "He won't sleep if he doesn't have his carrot blanket in his pen, you know."

"Right," Ellie said, like she had known this.

"Plus, he usually gets four yogurt treats every morning, and he didn't get any this morning. So he's hungry for those, too."

"Of course," Kit said.

Melody stood still for a long time then said, "Mom said we could go to the pet store to get another rabbit and try to use him in my magic act. That way I still do my magic act instead of my gymnastics routine. It's probably the best thing to do, since everyone likes an act with a rabbit onstage."

"It *is* a good act with a rabbit," Kit said, nodding. "I've always thought it was very impressive."

Melody inhaled. "Except a new rabbit would probably just ruin the hat. It was very expensive, and Pancakes was very well trained, you know. He really felt at home in that hat, sort of the same way I feel at home wearing my crown. So I think it's a bad idea to get a new rabbit. It'd be better to just find Pancakes."

Ellie looked at Kit. Kit looked at Toby. They all knew what Melody was trying hard to *not* say: that she didn't want a new rabbit, and it wasn't really because of an expensive hat. Melody wanted Pancakes back because he was her pet, and she loved him exactly the way you're supposed to love your pets. Ellie thought it was sort of sad that Melody didn't want to say that outright, but she knew some people weren't so good at explaining how they felt, especially if they felt sad. Sad was just such a tricky thing to explain.

"What about me?" Toby asked helpfully.

Melody narrowed her eyes. "What *about* you?"

"Maybe I could help with your magic act! That'd be extremely congenial. I probably won't fit in a hat, but what if you sawed me in half?"

Melody scowled, but it was a thoughtful kind of scowl. Then she said, "That's not really part of my magic act. But that would be very impressive."

"I'm very symmetrical. I bet that's good for sawing tricks," Toby said.

Melody looked like she might be seriously considering this, then she shook her head. "No—it's too late to change my magic act that much. I'll just hope your *contraption* catches

Pancakes tonight or that the thief is caught." Melody didn't sound quite so mean when she said it this time—it was more like she was just saying it out of habit. "I'm in room 304, if that *thing* works."

"Okay! We'll come get you if we catch him!" Ellie assured Melody as she walked away. Ellie looked at Toby and frowned. "Hey—how come you never offered to let me saw you in half for my talent? That would be way better than ballet!"

"Because I think *you'd* use a real saw," Toby said, shivering. "And I'm not *that* congenial."

After they finished eating and the server assured Ellie that the rabbit catcher was still empty, they all went back to their hotel rooms. Hotels always had really good movies, so Ellie found three different ones she liked and flipped back and forth among them while her mom worked on Ellie's pageant dress (Ellie's mom *really* couldn't stop sewing).

"Okay, I'm done. I think. Maybe? What do you think?" Ellie's mom asked, holding up the dress. It was so covered in ruffles and beads and sequins that you could hardly even see the dress underneath all the decorations.

"I *think* I should go check on my rabbit catcher before bed," Ellie said, and then quickly added, "and also that it looks great."

"It *does*, doesn't it?" Ellie's mom said, admiring the dress. "And you know I've already answered that question about the rabbit catcher, Ellie."

Ellie sighed. Her mom refused to answer questions twice. She said it was in a parenting policy she'd signed, but Ellie was almost sure that wasn't true. Ellie's mom said that she couldn't very well go prowling around by the trash bins at night looking for a rabbit— that it wasn't safe. Ellie tried to explain that she'd already *been* to the kitchen, and knew it was very clean, and that trash bins probably were safer than cars but they got in the car almost every day—

But then Ellie's mom had given her *the look*, and Ellie had gone back to watching her movies.

"I think your ballet routine will look very nice tomorrow," her mom said. "Are you excited?"

Ellie nodded. "Yes. Sort of. I still just wish I had a cooler talent!"

"You have a *very* cool talent, Ellie! You're the only elementary school engineer I know," her mom said.

"But that's not what I'm doing onstage," Ellie said. "I just wish I had a talent that was good for showing off." She didn't say it out loud, but she also couldn't stop thinking about all the things Melody had said about engineering. Just because Ellie had decided to help Melody didn't mean all the teasing didn't still bother her. Was engineering not as cool as she'd always thought?

Ellie's mom frowned then put the dress aside. She patted the spot on the bed beside her. Ellie got up and sat down, scooching so her purple leopard-spot nightgown wasn't scrunched up under her.

"Just because a talent isn't good onstage doesn't mean it's not special, Ellie. What if someone's talent is reading very fast? Or writing great poems? Or knowing the perfect thing to say when someone is sad? A *stage* is just a bunch of wood all nailed together—"

"I think they used screws," Ellie said thoughtfully.

"Okay, screwed together—my point is, Ellie, that a stage isn't a real place. It's for looking at and is awfully fun to dance around on, but the way you use your talents *off* the stage, when lots of people *aren't* looking, is way more important than anything you do on it. Do you understand?"

Ellie huffed a little then kicked her legs against the mattress. "I understand."

Her mom nodded and went on. "*And* there's nothing wrong with doing something just for fun, even if it isn't your best talent. Like, say . . . making a pageant dress," she said, prodding the pile of fabric. "I know that making dresses isn't my talent—but I like doing it."

"You're really good at it. No one else's dress has so many sparkles," Ellie said.

"You'll shine!" Ellie's mom said, then she tilted her head. "You know, this side has one more ruffle than the other. I oughta add another to that part so it's even."

Chapter Twelve

Ellie woke up extra early the next morning. At first she thought it was because the bed was a little weird and too soft, but then she realized it was because her brain had gotten all ready to check the rabbit catcher while her body was still asleep. She sat up straight and looked over at her mom next to her. (There were two beds in the hotel room, but on the first night Ellie had decided that sleeping by herself in a giant bed was lonely.)

"Mom," she whispered. "It's morning."

"Mmmfffreee," her mom said.

"Can I go check my rabbit catcher, since it's not night?"

"Eeeeeeee," her mom said, but maybe it was a really wheezy snore. Ellie decided that was good enough, though, and slipped on her sneakers and tool belt then hurried downstairs. She was still in her purple leopard nightgown, but that was basically a dress, wasn't it? Besides, she was just going to check the rabbit catcher and run right back upstairs.

The hotel was very empty this early in the morning, save for a few people in suits and dress shirts hurrying in and out of the main door. The people behind the front desk tilted their heads at her when she walked past, so she waved like she thought Toby would then kept going. There weren't many people in the hotel restaurant just yet; there was a woman setting up a big table of bagels and juices and a griddle to make eggs on, but other than her, it was empty. Ellie marched straight to the kitchen doors, pushed them open, and hurried toward the trash bins and the rabbit catcher.

Please please please please please be in the trap, Pancakes, she thought as loudly as she could while walking up to the trap. She gasped when she saw movement ahead—was that him? Had she arrived just moments before he hopped into her rabbit catcher? She ran the last few steps—

It wasn't Pancakes—it wasn't even a rabbit at all! It was—

"Melody?" Ellie asked, her voice louder than she meant it to be.

"What? Who? Yes!" Melody shouted, springing awake. Ellie leaped back; Melody leaped to her feet; they both stared at each other, wide-eyed and alarmed.

"Were you asleep?" Ellie asked, confused. Melody's hair was ruffled up on one side, and there were pillow lines on her face. She wasn't wearing her crown, either, though Ellie saw it was right by Melody's feet.

"No! Who sleeps next to a trash bin? Why would you think that?" Melody scoffed.

Ellie looked at Melody's feet, then she pointed to the pillow and blanket on the ground. "But . . ."

Melody bit her lip. She breathed in through her nose in a way that reminded Ellie of the way bulls do in cartoons, right before they charge you. For a moment, she wondered what she should do if Melody charged at her.

But instead of charging, Melody's brown eyes welled up with tears.

"I just wanted to make sure I was here if Pancakes showed up," she said as the tears began to drip-drop down her cheeks. "It was really clever, thinking he might come to eat the vegetables, so I snuck out and came down to wait, but he never came."

"Oh, oh," Ellie said, wishing that she had the talent her mom had thought of last night—knowing the perfect thing to say when someone is sad. "Maybe he's . . . um . . . maybe he's busy and running late?"

Ellie cringed, because that might very well have been the *least* perfect thing to say.

But Melody didn't seem to notice how least perfect Ellie's words were; she said, sniffling, "No—he isn't here because of me. It's my fault!"

"It's not your fault, Melody! Sometimes pets just get lost, and sometimes it's extra hard to find them. But we'll leave the trap here and—"

"No," Melody said, stamping her foot angrily. "It's my fault because I left the cage door open!"

Ellie's eyes went big. She didn't say anything because she didn't know *what* to say to this.

Melody kept going, wiping at her face with

the bottom of her palm. "When I went to play with him after leaving the pool, I put him in the cage but didn't close the door because I just meant to leave for a second, while I went to put my pajamas on for the pajama party. But then I started talking to Emily about putting on mascara, and then I wanted to show two of the girls from the little kids division my crown, and then I started to go to the pajama party, and when I remembered and hurried back, Pancakes was *gone*." By the time Melody was finished speaking, her face was all covered in tears again, plus her nose was running and she was hiccupping a little. It was all very un-Melody-like.

Ellie decided that even though she wasn't sure what to say, she was sure what to do—she stepped up and hugged Melody really tightly, the way her grandmother hugged her when Ellie was sad about going home after their beach vacation was finished. Melody cried harder and hugged her back and kept talking about Pancakes, but it was impossible for Ellie to know what she was saying, since her face was buried against Ellie's leopard nightgown.

Finally, Melody sniffled and put her head back up. Her cheeks were red, and her eyes were tiny because they were puffy from all the crying. "I'm sorry I blamed Kit when I knew it wasn't her fault."

"That's something you need to say to Kit," Ellie told her. "But I know she'll forgive you. That's just how Kit is."

"I know. I'll tell her I'm sorry. I just didn't want people to know I'd been so forgetful. What kind of Miss Junior Peachy Keen loses her talent *and* her pet? We brought my magician stuff all the way here, and now it's just going to sit in the prop room and *no one* will get to see the new sparkly jacket I got. And now I'm going to be in trouble for leaving the room and for waking my mom up when I knock to get back inside because I *also* forgot the little key! My mom does *not* like to be woken up, especially before eight o'clock," Melody said, snatching her crown off the floor and situating it on her head. It was a touch crooked, but Ellie knew better than to mention this.

Instead, Ellie pressed her lips together and thought very hard. "It's almost seven o'clock. What if we waited for Pancakes till eight o'clock, when your mom wakes up, then went back to the room together?"

Melody sniffed so hard it was more like a snort, then she shook her head. "People will be awake at eight o'clock, and they'll make fun of me for crying."

"Anyone who makes fun of someone for crying isn't a very nice person," Ellie said, but she understood—Kit didn't like for people to see her cry, either. "Let's think. There must be a way back into the room without waking up your mom."

Ellie thought about the door on the hotel room and the way it opened on the inside. It wasn't all that tricky, really—she just needed to turn the knob from the inside, and it would open right up. But how . . . ?

"I've got it!" Ellie said.

"Got what?" Melody sniffed.

"A way for you to get back into your room! Come on—you'll need to help."

Melody looked quite confused but followed behind Ellie anyhow as they left the kitchen.

"We need to find a coat hanger and some-thing in a circle. Any ideas?" Ellie asked.

"The ladies who sell T-shirts in the pageant room had coat hangers. I bet there's one by their booth," Melody said.

"Perfect! Go get one and meet me back

here," Ellie told her. Melody hurried away, and Ellie started hunting for the other piece she needed—some sort of circle, like a teeny Hula-Hoop. She walked around the dining room and the lobby, and then back toward the area where the lady was setting up breakfast.

There it was!

"Excuse me," Ellie said in her most polite voice. She reached out for a handshake, Toby style. The lady shook her hand, a little startled. Ellie went on. "I'm Ellie, engineer, and can you tell me what those are?"

"These? These are just eggs," the lady said, motioning to the basket of bright-white eggs on the table.

"No, no—those," Ellie said, and pointed to some little silver rings, about the size of her hand.

"Oh! These are for cooking eggs. It keeps them from running everywhere in the pan," the lady said. "Did you want an egg, sweetie?"

"No, I think eggs smell like feet," Ellie said, then realized this might not be polite, so she added, "I'm sure your eggs don't. And that your feet don't smell, either. I just wondered if I could borrow one of those rings? I'll return it really quickly!"

The lady frowned, like she didn't understand.

"It'd be awfully congenial of you," Ellie added.

The lady kept frowning, but then she shrugged and handed Ellie one of the rings. Ellie grinned, thanked the lady, and then sprinted back to where she'd last seen Melody. Melody was on her way back, too, holding a coat hanger.

"How will this help?" Melody asked. "And how will *that* help? Are we making eggs? Are we going to try to bribe someone to open the door for us with eggs? Because I'm not a very good cook."

"Nope—we're going to build something," Ellie said, grinning. She pulled out her notepad and began to draw.

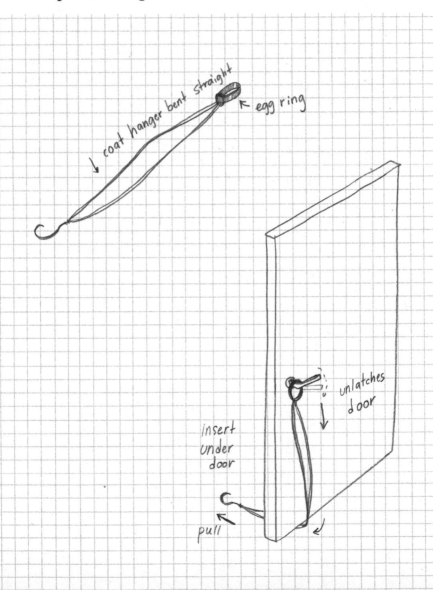

It took no time at all for Ellie to bend up the coat hanger and attach it to the egg circle. She carefully slid it under the door, rotated it, and then pushed it up, up, up until she felt the egg circle hit the handle.

"Got it!" Ellie said triumphantly.

"Shhhh," Melody said, elbowing her. "My mom's asleep, remember?"

"Oh, right," Ellie said. "Got it!" she whispered. She wiggled the coat hanger hook around a little until she felt the egg circle slide over the handle, then she tugged down. The handle turned! The door clicked, and just like that, it pushed open!

"Wow!" Melody said. "I guess this is why hotels have those big inside-only locks, too, right?"

"Yes, but *shhhh*—your mom's asleep, remember?" Ellie said, then laughed a little. Melody laughed, too, and Ellie really wanted to tell

Melody that she should try to laugh more often, because it was really nice to hear. She also really wanted to ask Melody if she *still* thought engineering was weird, since it was really saving her bacon right now, but she didn't, since she was a little afraid Melody would tell her that yes, it was still weird.

"See you at the pageant! Good luck!" Ellie said as Melody slipped inside.

"You too," Melody said, and Ellie felt like she might really mean it.

Chapter Thirteen

When Ellie got back to her own room, her mom was already awake and not terribly pleased to hear that Ellie had snuck down to the kitchen to check the rabbit catcher. She softened a little bit when Ellie told her about Melody being there.

"I do wish you'd caught the rabbit," Ellie's mom said with a sigh. "Melody and her mother are a bit . . . well . . . *competitive*, but I still never like when someone loses a pet. Now, come on— if you want your hair in a bun for the ballet routine, you know I need to start now."

It was true—Ellie's mom was good at buns, but only if she had a very long time to do them. Ellie sat on the floor while her mom combed and slicked and gelled her hair, and by nine o'clock, she was finished. Ellie and Kit's division started right at nine, which gave Ellie just enough time to finally add the switch to Kit's lights! Kit was already in her skateboarding gear and looked great—Ellie just knew she would be the star of the talent show, and she told Kit that.

"Thanks," Kit said, then motioned at Ellie's ballet outfit. "Your tutu looks beautiful, too!" Then, a little quieter, Kit added, "I guess the rabbit catcher didn't work, by the way? No Pancakes?"

"No Pancakes," Ellie said, shaking her head.

"I guess finding a missing rabbit was just too much luck to ask from my necklace," Kit said, swirling her finger around her coin necklace.

Ellie touched her own necklace. She hadn't told Kit or Toby about seeing Melody that morning. She didn't usually keep secrets from her best friends, but Melody had been so worried about people seeing her crying that this felt like the kind of secret you should keep. Besides, Melody was still going to come clean about blaming Kit for Pancakes, wasn't she? But when? It didn't seem fair to make Kit wait all day, especially when the pageant ended this afternoon.

"Come on," Ellie said, wanting to think about something other than Pancakes. "Let's go add the switch to the lights!"

They made their way to the area just outside the prop storage room, where everyone's talent props were lined up, ready to be brought backstage. Ellie knew exactly how to add a switch to the lights, so she wasn't worried about doing it so last minute—in fact, she'd left her tool belt upstairs and brought down only the tools she needed for the lights. Ellie explained it all to Kit and Toby while she worked.

"So, remember how you need the current to go in a circle to make the lights work?" Ellie asked, even though it was the sort of question that you didn't really expect an answer to. "We're going to put a switch right . . . here." She lifted her pair of sharp pliers (she'd had to listen to a *lot* of rules about using these when her dad got them for her) and snipped the wire for the lights in half. Kit yelped.

"You broke the circle!" she said, and Ellie knew that she was nervous *and* pretending not to be.

"We don't have very long, Ellie," Toby added, and he wasn't nearly as good at pretending to not be nervous as Kit.

"Right—but I'm going to fix the circle by putting this in!" Ellie said, and held up a tiny little switch. She'd taken it off a toy that lit up and buzzed and didn't stop lighting up and buzzing until her mom threatened to throw it out the window but wound up just taking the batteries out. It hadn't been a very good toy, really, but it had really good *parts*, so Ellie had taken it apart and kept all the pieces for other builds. She stuck the wires into the switch, and the lights came back on!

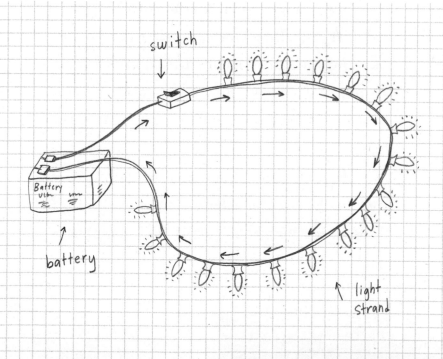

"Whew," Kit said.

"I knew it would work," Toby said (he wasn't good at this pretending, either).

"So when you flip the switch, it breaks the circuit on purpose to turn off the lights. All lights work like this! It's just like a light switch on the wall," Ellie explained, grinning. "Now it's easier to turn the lights on once you're onstage, instead of having to wire it all up to the battery every time you want them to come on!"

"This is going to be so amazing," Kit said, and hugged Ellie tightly. It felt like she was hugging Ellie not just for the lights and the switch but also for how hard Ellie tried to find Pancakes, so Ellie hugged her back just as hard.

A big round of applause from the pageant room came out of nowhere—

"Oh, it's 9:17—that means that clapping is

for Emily! I hope she didn't drop any batons," Kit said, pulling back and clapping her hands together even though Emily wouldn't have been able to hear it from the pageant room.

"Wow," Toby said as they wheeled the ramp back up against the wall, where it would wait till Kit was ready. "There must be a lot of people in there." He looked back at Ellie and Kit and seemed worried. "Are you scared?"

"Of what?" Ellie asked.

"All the people. Looking at you," Toby said. "With their eyes."

Ellie considered this. "Only a little. Someone is always looking at someone, and it's almost always with their eyes."

"Still," Toby said warily. "That's a lot of eyes. I bet there's at least two hundred eyeballs in there."

"Sometimes I do get stage fright," Kit admitted. "Not so much anymore, but when I was first doing pageants, one time I ran off the stage and over to my mom right in front of everyone. I bet I'd have run all the way home if I could have."

"Oh, yes," Toby said, nodding. "That's called *fight, flight, or freeze.* When you get scared or startled, your body goes *oh my gosh* and you feel like you either need to fight something or run someplace safe or just go super still!"

Kit tilted her head to the side in thought. "Hmm. I wonder what would happen if my body decided to fight when I got scared. I probably wouldn't still be doing pageants, that's for sure. I bet fighting the judges isn't— Ellie? Where are you going?"

Ellie was running away, shocked that she hadn't thought of this before! Could it really be so simple?

Without stopping, she called over her shoulder, "I have an idea! We have to flight like Pancakes!"

Kit and Toby looked at each other, each hoping the other understood. Neither did, but they took off after Ellie anyhow, since that's what friends do. Ellie ran through the lobby, down the short hall, to the prop storage room.

Where is it? It had to be in here somewhere; Melody had said it herself— "There! Right there!" Ellie said, pointing. Melody's magician routine props! They were tucked away in the corner, unused—an abracadabra wand, the bunch of rainbow-colored handkerchiefs, the juggling balls, and the— *Yes!* The costume with the top hat.

"Why do we need Melody's stuff?" Toby asked as Ellie wove around some Hula-Hoops, a whole bunch of wigs, and some very fancy-looking stilts.

"Not her stuff—her hat!" Ellie said, reaching the magician props. She held her breath. *Please be right, please be right, please be right,* she thought as hard as she could. Then Ellie stooped down and picked up the top hat.

It was heavy. *Too* heavy for a plain old hat.

Ellie grinned then hugged the hat to her chest. She tipped it just a little so that Toby and Kit could see what was inside.

"Oh my gosh," Toby said, slapping his hand to his forehead.

"I can't believe it!" Kit squealed, bouncing on her heels.

Nestled in the hat, looking very sleepy and very confused, was none other than Pancakes.

Chapter Fourteen

"How in the world did he end up *here*?" Toby asked. "And how did you know he'd be here?"

Ellie reached down and patted Pancakes's rabbit head. He was very soft and made little rabbit sniffly noises at her. "It was half what Kit said—that she got so scared she'd have run home if she could have—and half what Melody said that first night, that it took months and months for Pancakes to feel at home in this hat."

"He came home," Kit said. "Wow. Way to go, Pancakes."

Pancakes didn't seem particularly impressed with himself, but rabbits never were.

A round of applause from the main pageant stage nabbed their attention, and then the announcer's voice: "Thank you so much, Miss Piper Pellegrin! Those spins sure were fast, huh, folks? Up next: last year's Miss Junior Peachy Keen champion, Miss Melody Harris!"

Ellie, Toby, and Kit all looked at one another with giant eyes. Melody was going on to do her gymnastics routine! But Pancakes was right here—

"Run!" Kit said, and Ellie didn't have to be told twice. She cradled the hat and bolted back through the prop room, down the hall, into the ballroom, and behind the curtains that led up to the stage. Melody's gymnastics routine was seconds from starting, but the music hadn't begun—there was still time for her to be a magician, still time for her to pull Pancakes out of the hat, *go, go, go faster, Ellie, faster!* Kit's mom was at the side of the stage with Kit's skateboarding ramp, looking very unhappy about the fact that Ellie was sprinting toward her while Kit, who was to go on very soon, was nowhere in sight.

"Ellie! *Where* is Kit—"

"One moment, please!" Ellie said, then took the steps to the stage in two big jumps.

She skidded to a stop.

Ellie squinted. The lights were bright, and they were shining right on her. She looked out and realized that there were definitely two hundred eyeballs, if not more, in the audience. And that she was onstage in a ballet costume, when it was most definitely *not* her turn.

"Sorry," she whispered to no one in particular. The whisper caught Melody's attention. She'd been posed in a very dramatic and very bendy opening position, but now that she saw Ellie walking toward her, she sat up and, with a smile and little curtsy at the baffled judges, darted over to her.

"What's going on?" Melody said, and she sounded a bit like the old Melody—which is to say, she sounded very annoyed with Ellie.

"Sorry to interrupt," Ellie whispered, and turned her back to the audience. She held out the hat so that only Melody could see—

Melody made a little happy sound, then she leaped up and down, clapping her hands to her mouth. She snatched the hat away from Ellie and hugged it tightly just as Toby and Kit panted onto the stage with the rainbow handkerchiefs, the juggling balls, the abracadabra wand—all the things Melody needed to do her magician act.

One of the pageant ladies was walking up to the stage, her high heels click-clacking on the wood as she went. (Ellie happened to look down and notice that she'd been right earlier—they had used *screws* and not nails on the stage! She'd have to remember to tell her mom—)

"Ladies and . . . young man," she said, glancing at Toby.

"Toby Michaels, your future Miss Congeniality," Toby said, handing the handkerchiefs to Kit so he could offer the lady a handshake.

"Erm, yes," she said, shaking his hand. "Is everything all right? We need to move along."

Melody looked at Ellie then at Kit, and Ellie was very, very sure that Melody was going to apologize. She was going to tell Kit about everything—about how she'd been the one to leave the cage open and how she'd known all along that Kit hadn't sabotaged her! She was going to fix it all, and everyone was going to be happy because Pancakes was back!

But then Melody looked to the lady and just said, "Yes—but I'm going to do my original magician's routine."

"Oh! How lovely," the woman said. "Well, let's get on with it, then, all right? This is counting toward your two and a half minutes."

"Right, right," Melody said. She grabbed her props and hustled to place them in the right spots. Ellie, Kit, and Toby hustled off the stage.

"What is going on?" Kit's mom asked.

"Pancakes! Ellie found him!" Kit said excitedly.

Ellie wasn't surprised that Kit was so excited—Kit was very nice that way. Still, Ellie couldn't help but feel a little angry that Melody hadn't apologized to Kit, not even when she had Pancakes back in her arms. She thought about what Melody had told her that morning—that she didn't want people to know she'd lost Pancakes, since Miss Junior Peachy Keen shouldn't lose her talent like that. Was that why Melody hadn't said anything? Did she not want anyone to know because she thought winning was more important?

That didn't seem very right.

"Ellie! Ellie, did you hear me?" a voice—Kit's voice!—said.

"What is it?" Ellie asked, spinning around just as Melody's magic act began.

Kit looked panicked. She pointed at the ramp. "The lights aren't coming on anymore. It's broken!"

Chapter Fifteen

"It was just working—I tested it in the hall before they moved it in here!" Kit's mom said in a very stern voice. "If the lights don't work, we ought to pull them off. If she goes up there, and there are lights that don't turn on, it'll be worse than no lights at all."

"Ellie can fix it, Mom. Give her a minute!" Kit said, though she looked very, very worried that this wasn't true. Melody's routine was almost over—she hadn't even had her whole two and a half minutes, after all. And as soon as Melody finished, it was Ellie's turn then Kit's. How could Ellie fix the lights if she had to be onstage at the same time?

Let's think. You can do this, Ellie Bell, Ellie told herself. She reached for her tool belt—

She gasped.

She wasn't wearing her tool belt—she was wearing a tutu. She hadn't put on her tool belt with her ballet costume, since it would have smashed down all the fluffy tutu parts. The only tool she had was the wire clippers she'd used to add the switch—and she'd left those in the hallway.

"Ellie?" Kit asked nervously. Her mom already had a hand on one string of lights, ready to yank.

"Okay," Ellie said, thinking out loud. Thinking out loud was something her dad did a lot, and she'd started doing it without really meaning to. "There must just be a break in the circuit. Circuits have to go in a whole circle to work—we just need to find the break!"

"That was last year's Miss Junior Peachy Keen, Melody Harris!" the announcer said. "Up next, we have Miss Ellie Bell, performing a ballet dance."

"Quick, help me pull them off!" Kit's mom said frantically.

"No! No," Ellie said, taking big deep breaths. "I have an idea. Help me push the ramp onto the stage."

"But it isn't my turn yet, Ellie. It's yours. You need to go—hurry, before you lose your time," Kit said, looking sad. All that work to help with Melody's act, and it was Kit's that wound up being ruined!

Ellie chewed her lip. She had an idea. It was the sort of idea that might be a great one or might be a terrible one, and she couldn't really say for sure which it was. She knew this much, though—that she was the *only* one who could get the lights fixed before Kit's performance.

"Push the ramp out onto the stage!" Ellie said hurriedly.

"But wait, it's not my turn yet—" Kit said.

"Let's go people, move, move, we've got a schedule to keep!" Toby said, and began shuffling Kit's mom and the pageant people and even a few of the other girls waiting to go onstage. "Punctuality is very congenial!" he added, just in case anyone thought differently.

Kit's mom looked like she was very unsure about what was happening, but everyone else started moving so quickly that she didn't have time to argue. The pageant people wheeled Kit's skateboarding ramp onto the stage, and Ellie followed before her body could decide to do that whole *fight, flight, freeze* thing that Toby had told her about. Ellie looked out into the audience and saw her mom, who seemed a little confused but clapped really, really loudly anyway.

"Miss Ellie Bell, who will be performing a dance routine to 'Pachelbel's Canon'—"

"Wait!" Ellie said, interrupting. The judges all looked up, and Ellie worried that might have been rude, so she smiled her best pageant smile (she and Kit had been practicing it at home, and a perfect pageant smile was harder than you'd think). Ellie padded over to the announcer in her ballet slippers. "For my talent, I will be repairing the lights on my best friend Kit's skateboarding ramp." She paused and then quickly added, "While ballet dancing."

"Oh!" the audience said, some nodding, some tilting their heads the way Kit's pet sheep did when she heard a new sound. Ellie felt her stomach go wobbly. Sure, the judges had told her that helping someone was *never* embarrassing, but she couldn't get over how she'd never seen a single other pageant girl engineer onstage—it just didn't seem like a flashy, showy pageant talent! Maybe the dancing-while-engineering part would help, though. Right?

Right.

Ellie's whole body felt wobbly now, and she really, *really* hoped she was right. She stepped away from the announcer and put her arms over her head in the opening pose for her ballet routine. There wasn't any music now, so she just played it in her head and spun around in a circle, then jumped/hopped/pranced toward the ramp.

"Electricity!" Ellie said as she bounced to the ramp. "It comes in two types—current and static!" She waved to one side for the word "current" and the other for the word "static." "Current has to go around in a circle. The electricity goes out the plug or the battery and into the wires, then through the thing you're giving electricity to, then back down into the plug. A circle!"

She spun in a circle, then another, just to make sure everyone understood. She wanted to do a few more, but this was starting to make her super dizzy. "These lights won't turn on because the circle is broken. But they can be fixed! We just need to find the spot where the wire is cut, or bent, or broken apart!"

Someone in the audience cheered—wait, no! It wasn't someone in the audience at all. It was the group of people standing backstage— the other pageant girls and Kit and Toby and even Kit's mom! They cheered so loudly that the audience started clapping, too. Ellie felt her heart fill up like a balloon—maybe this wasn't going too badly!

She jumped and twirled as prettily as she could over to one side of the ramp, sweeping her eyes along the string of lights. "No breaks here!" she announced.

The crowd cheered again.

She twirled and even stopped to do a dance step she really loved that looked like the way a cat jumps, then she peered over the middle of the ramp. "No breaks here, either!" she told the crowd.

"Find it!" someone yelled.

"Where is it?" someone else yelled.

"Ellie can fix anything!" someone else yelled, and Ellie was 90 percent sure this was her mom.

Finally, Ellie danced over to the other side of the ramp, stopped, and did a plié and a nice rond de jambe, just like she'd learned in ballet class. She peered at the lights that went across the top of the ramp, and—

"It's here!" she said.

Everyone cheered, especially the people backstage. Kit's mom looked a little sweaty. Ellie reached down and tugged on the wires to connect them back together—

Her heart sank.

There was just no way to do it, though—the wire was already pulled tight so that Kit's skateboard didn't get caught in it, like it had during their test run back home! If she had a bit of wire from her tool belt. Or maybe a piece of aluminum foil! Or even a fork—

But she didn't have any of those things. Who brings a fork onstage for a ballet/engineering talent performance?

Ellie swallowed. Now she was only going to be a so-so dancer *and* a so-so engineer onstage, and Kit's lights weren't even going to work for the trouble. She turned to the audience and tried to do the cat jump again, but it was clumsy, and she almost hurt her ankle.

"The wires won't reach," she said, trying to explain and dance at once. It wasn't working very well at all, and she knew her time had to be almost up. Ellie looked offstage at Kit, who was smiling. Kit wouldn't be mad at her if the lights didn't get fixed. Kit was nice like that. "We need something to complete the circuit, but I don't have anything that will work," Ellie said, and even though she was on the stage, she was talking mostly to Kit.

"But I do!" a new voice said, and it was *loud*. Really loud, and sort of singsongy, and coming from the opposite side of the stage. Ellie whirled around (remembering at the very last second to make it a dance-whirl instead of a surprise-whirl).

It was Melody! Smiling big, facing the audience, and looking very, very fancy as she stepped out onto the stage. Lots of people clapped for her, though there was also a lot of confused talking going on—people whispering and wondering and pointing.

"Will this work, Miss Bell?" Melody asked, twirling toward Ellie with a very fancy spin that Ellie didn't know how to do.

"It— Oh!" Ellie said when she realized what

Melody was holding. "*This?*" she asked, looking up at Melody.

Melody nodded and waved the object a little, urging Ellie to take it. She flashed another smile at the audience. "Let's see her fix it!" Melody shouted to the people. "Let's see Ellie engineer!"

The audience cheered. Ellie felt the way her stuffed monkey looked when he was going round and round in the dryer—because the thing that Melody was waving at Ellie, trying to get her to take? Was her *crown*.

Whoa.

Ellie took the crown from Melody's hands as carefully as she could. "Thank you, Melody!" she said loudly, though she was still so surprised by all this that her voice was a little squeaky. "We can try using this to complete the circuit!"

"Fix it! Fix it! Fix it!" Melody began to

chant, and the crowd did, too, and so did all the girls backstage and *even the judges.*

Ellie grabbed the ends of the light wires and wrapped them around the two sides of the crown's headband. She then jumped up and ran to the switch she'd put in just that morning; she flipped it on.

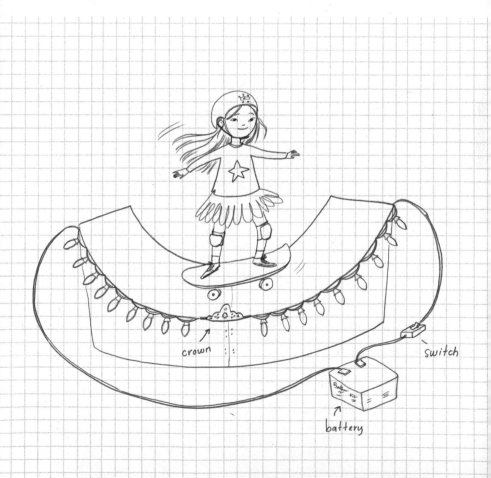

crown

switch

battery

The audience gasped then applauded.

Ellie looked at Melody, who grinned back at her.

The circuit was complete—and the lights were on.

The announcer's voice boomed out. "Next up, Miss Katherine Yoshimoto, performing a skateboarding routine—on a pretty amazing ramp, no less!"

Chapter Sixteen

Kit skateboarded like a skateboarding pro, if you asked Ellie. She *whoosh*ed up and down the ramp, dodging Melody's crown and jumping into the air at the edges, so you could see the purple otters she'd drawn on the bottom side of the board. She was a ball of pink clothes and black hair, and every time she landed back on the board, the audience exploded with cheers. It was basically the best thing Ellie had ever seen, or at least the best skateboarding she'd ever seen, and she'd watched a *lot* of skateboarding videos with Kit.

That afternoon was the very last part of the pageant, when everyone wore their fancy dresses and walked onstage and waved like they were a queen or boss or president. Ellie walked in her high-heeled shoes with her balancers, and Melody and Kit and most everyone else walked in their high-heeled shoes without balancers. Ellie was pretty sure her dress weighed about a billion pounds, what with all the sparkles and sequins and beads and ruffles on it, but she was also pretty sure it was the best thing she'd worn in her whole entire life. (Which was really saying something, since she'd worn a ninja duck costume last Halloween.)

They stood in their very certain lines at the back of the stage, and after a whole bunch of announcements about more pageants and companies that had paid money to be talked about and someone in a green car whose lights were on, it was time for the awards. All the air around Ellie felt the way she figured one light in a circuit felt—with lots of buzzing electricity on both sides and you in the middle. Thinking about *that* made Ellie wonder about what it felt like for a light when you turned it off and all that electricity went away. Was it like taking a nap? Maybe—

"And the winner of the Miss Congeniality award, voted on by her fellow contestants, is . . . ," the pageant person said. Everyone kept smiling. Ellie's cheeks were starting to hurt—even for someone who smiled a lot, like she did, this was a *lot* of smiling—

"Contestant number thirty-two, Miss Ellie Bell!"

Ellie thought for a moment. That sounded just like her name! Maybe the acoustics in this room weren't very good. She'd read all about acoustics and how sound bounced off some things better than it bounced off other things.

"Ellie!" Kit said.

Ellie turned and looked at Kit, confused— they weren't supposed to talk onstage, and Kit hardly ever broke rules that were written down like that.

"Go!" Kit whisper-shouted, waving her arms.

And then Melody was doing the same thing! And then Emily, and Sarah, and—

"Oh!" Ellie realized.

She stepped forward, wobbling a little despite her heel balancers, and walked to the front of the stage. An older girl with bright-red hair put a sash around Ellie's shoulders, one that said Miss Congeniality in big black letters. *Voted on by her fellow contestants!* They'd decided she was the most congenial! Ellie turned back around and looked at the girls onstage, who were clapping and smiling and all looking very beautiful and fancy and pageant-y.

"Really?" Ellie asked as she walked back to her spot in line.

Sarah, who was standing next to her, laughed, then she whispered, "Of course! You helped a bunch of us with our talents. *And* you found Pancakes! *And* you saved Kit's lights! I'd have voted for you even if Melody hadn't told us all to!"

"Melody said to vote for me?" Ellie asked. Her eyebrows tried to go up when she said this, but Kit's mom had used some sort of weird paste or glue or grease on Ellie's brows, so they couldn't move much at all.

Sarah frowned, considering. "I really think *told* is the better word. Melody can be a little demanding, you know."

Melody didn't look demanding right now, though—she looked happy. She was still clapping for Ellie, maybe louder than everyone else combined. Even louder than Kit, who was just about glowing with excitement! Ellie and Kit distance-high-fived behind everyone's backs, which was where you did your hand like a high five but were too far away to actually touch, and then everyone went quiet again. It was time for the big award—for Miss Junior Peachy Keen to be announced.

The pageant person called out the second runner-up—Sarah, who got a small crown. And then the first runner-up—Kit!—who got a medium crown. When it came time to crown the new Miss Junior Peachy Keen, no one was very surprised to discover it was Melody. The pageant people had to help her put on a new ginormous crown, because it was so big that Melody wouldn't have been able to even hold it on her own. She waved at the audience, and loud music played, and then, just like that, parents in the audience were standing up to clap—then reaching around to grab all their empty chip bags and purses and phone chargers.

It was over!

Everyone on the stage rushed toward Melody to give her a hug and tell her congratulations. Kit was the first one to reach her— she was *very* fast in high heels, Ellie realized.

"I'm so happy for you!" Kit told Melody. "After you had such a lousy weekend looking for Pancakes!"

Melody was beaming, but her smile went a little different for a second. "Which—I knew you didn't take Pancakes, Kit. I'm sorry I said you did."

Kit shrugged. "That's okay."

"No, it isn't. It wasn't very Miss Junior Peachy Keen of me. I think it dishonored the crown," Melody said, shaking her head.

Emily gasped. Sarah put a hand to her mouth.

"No!" Piper said.

"What?" Ellie asked.

"You can't bring dishonor to the crown! Or you have to give it up!" Sarah whispered fearfully.

Melody hugged Kit again, and then bit her lip (without messing up her lipstick, which was impressive), like she was working up the courage to do something. Everyone crowded around her had gone still . . . until Melody reached up and carefully pulled the crown off her head. She stepped toward Kit, lifted the crown to Kit's fluffed-up hair, and—

"Congratulations, Melody," Kit said, reaching forward and grabbing Melody's hand. "I'm so glad you won!"

Everyone's eyes went big, but no one's went bigger than Melody's. Ellie watched as Melody put the crown back on her own head. Melody and Kit looked at each other for a few seconds, like they were having some sort of secret-eye-contact pageant conversation, and then Melody turned to Ellie.

"And Ellie? Your engineering ballet dance was *amazing*. Engineering is such a great talent. And I was just being mean when I made fun of engineering and said your tool belt looked grimy and all that other stuff. I'm really sorry."

"It *does* look a little grimy," Ellie admitted, though she was pink with happiness from the apology.

"No, no, it looks *vintage*," Melody corrected. "Vintage things are *supposed* to be grimy. It makes you very stylish."

"Oh! I didn't know that," Ellie said.

"I hope you come to another pageant—and if you do, I think it'd be really cool to help you engineer something, like Kit and that boy who kept offering me breath mints do. Would that be okay?" Melody asked, looking a little unsure. Ellie realized what she was really asking—if Ellie forgave her.

"That would be great," Ellie said, and Melody grinned before waving then walking off to rejoin her parents. Ellie and Kit linked arms and went to the edge of the stage, where their moms and Toby were waiting.

"Good game," Toby said, reaching out to shake Ellie's hand. "Finding Pancakes was extremely congenial, so I think that really got you ahead of me right there at the end."

"You were an excellent contestant, though," Ellie told him. "And I couldn't have found Pancakes without your help building the rabbit catcher."

Toby looked pleased, then he put a hand to his chin. "It's a shame we have to take it apart— but I promised the people at the desk that we'd give their table back."

"Nah, it's okay," Ellie said. "Besides—I know *just* what we'll build when we get home."

ELLIE BELL'S GUIDE TO ELECTRICITY*

*Electricity *can* be dangerous—I mean, most everything can be dangerous if you aren't careful. Electricity is extra dangerous sometimes, though, so be careful when you're learning about it.

ATOMS

To know about electricity, it helps a lot to know about atoms. *Everything* is made of atoms—you, your friends, your desk, your shoes, the trees, the moon, hot dogs, robots, swimming pools, *everything*. They're teeny-tiny, so it takes millions and billions of atoms to make stuff. Each atom has three parts: protons, neutrons, and electrons. They sort of look like this:

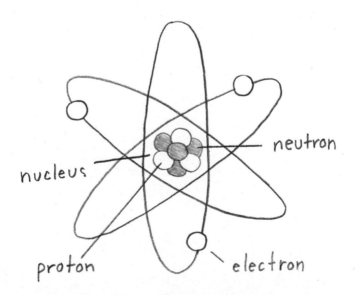

nucleus

neutron

proton

electron

In an atom, the electrons are the things that create electricity (which is easy to remember, since they both start with "elec"). An atom is happiest when it has the same number of protons and electrons—it just sits nicely, and nothing much happens. But when you *move* some of the electrons to a different atom? *That's* electricity!

TYPES OF ELECTRICITY

There are two types of electricity: static electricity and current electricity.

Static electricity is electricity that groups up all in one spot. Current electricity needs to flow along a path, like the way you run around the edge of the gym at school.

Here's an easy-peasy static electricity experiment:

1. Blow up a balloon.

2. Rub the balloon on your shirt for a few minutes. This knocks some of the electrons off the balloon and puts them in your body.

3. Hold the balloon to your hair. Your hair will stand up and stick to the balloon! This is because now the atoms in the balloon need electrons to be happy again, so your hair stands up to touch the balloon and give it electrons.

1.

2.

3.

Static electricity is fun, but current electricity is my favorite. Current electricity is how we power pretty much everything— cars, phones, lights, televisions, drills... *everything*. Current electricity needs to *flow* around a circle path called a circuit! *Circle, circuit?* See?

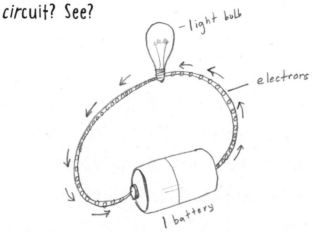

A circuit is a path for electrons to flow around and around, which is what gives us electrical power. The electrons leave the battery, go out and around the circuit and into the light, then back to the battery.

CONDUCTORS AND INSULATORS

Some materials make really good circuits, because they're great paths for electrons to travel on—like copper wire. These are called conductors.

Some materials make lousy circuits, because they're terrible paths for electrons to travel on—like rubber. These are called insulators. That's why when you see wire, sometimes it's wrapped in rubber—to keep the electrons on the circuit path!

If there's a break in the path, the electrons can't flow, so the electricity stops. A break in the path can happen by accident—like when the wire gets stepped on or sliced—or on purpose, like when you flip a light switch. A light switch works by breaking the circuit on purpose, which stops the flow of electrons!

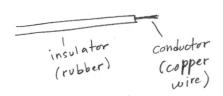

insulator
(rubber)

conductor
(copper
wire)

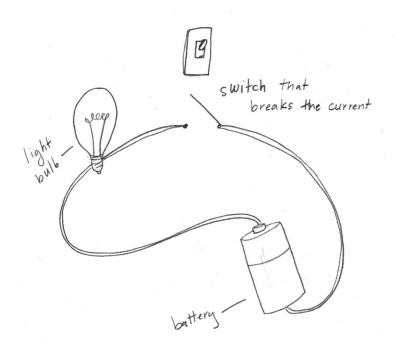

switch that
breaks the current

light
bulb

battery

AN EXPERIMENT WITH ELECTRICITY

Really, you're experimenting with electricity every single time you turn on a light—but there's an especially great way to play with current electricity that's really easy and fun. Here's what you do:

DOUGH CIRCUITS

You need:

• A battery holder with four AA batteries and a switch (you can buy one, but sometimes you can find one in an old toy to use!)

- LED lights (you need the little individual lights)

- 1 cup of flour (plus a little extra in a separate dish)

- 1 cup of water

- ¼ cup of salt

- 9 tablespoons of lemon juice

- 1 tablespoon of vegetable oil

- food coloring (I like purple, but you should pick your favorite color)

Mix the flour, water, salt, lemon juice, and vegetable oil in a saucepan. Put it on the stove over medium heat (you need an adult to help with this part) and stir, stir, stir

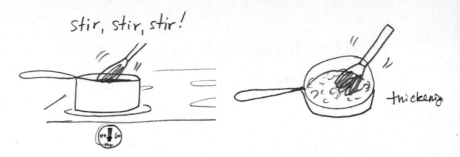

stir, stir, stir!

thickens

until it all gets thick and makes a big ball of dough. Then take it out of the pot and let it cool on the counter for a few minutes. Once it's cool, mash it up with a little extra flour until it isn't sticky anymore.

Now, roll out two little pieces of dough and put them beside each other but not touching. Poke one wire from your battery into one piece and the other wire into the other piece. Then stick the LED light in the middle of the two pieces of dough.

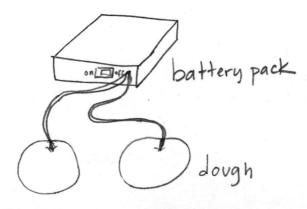

battery pack

dough

Turn on the switch! The electrons should be able to flow through the wire, into the dough, through the light, and then back to the batteries, making a perfect circuit—and the light should turn on!

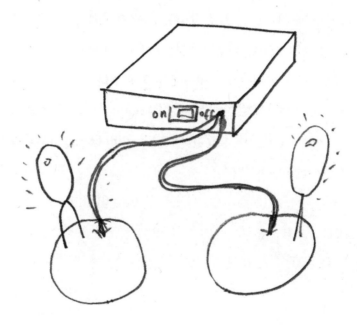

SHORT CIRCUITS

You can make the dough in a whole bunch of shapes. It won't work, though, if there isn't space between the two pieces of dough—if that happens, the electrical current will skip the light and go right to the other piece of dough then back into the battery. This is called a short circuit because the electrons take a *short*cut. Get it?

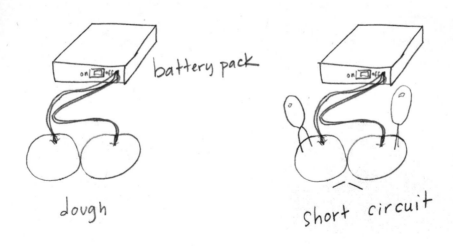

battery pack

dough

short circuit

HOW TO MAKE
INSULATING DOUGH

If you want to make something especially cool and need the two pieces of dough to touch, you can make a second kind of dough called insulating dough. (Remember: insulators are lousy paths for electricity! Electrons can't travel through this dough, so it can touch the other dough without causing a short circuit.)

INSULATING DOUGH

You need:

• 1 cup of flour

- ½ cup of sugar

- 3 tablespoons of vegetable oil

- ½ cup of water

- food coloring (choose a different color this time—I like pink or yellow for this one)

Stir it together until it becomes a big ball, then put it on the counter and mash it with some extra flour until it isn't sticky. That's it!

1.

stir

2.

3.

Take a little piece of this dough and put it between the other two pieces. The electrons can't get through this dough, so the circuit still works!

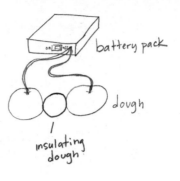

battery pack

dough

insulating dough

Here are some things I've made with squishy circuits!

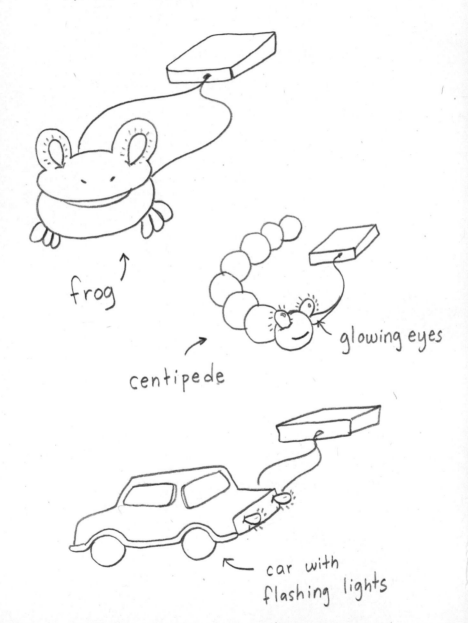

frog

centipede

glowing eyes

car with flashing lights